THE COMPENDIUM OF THE DEAD

Book 3 of The Papyrus Trilogy

Zoran Živković

FG-RS0024L5
ISBN: 978-4-908793-27-1

Cover: Youchan Ito, Togoru Art Works

Neoclassic Fleurons font
used with permission of Paulo W–Intellecta Design

Cadmus Press

cadmusmedia.org

THE COMPENDIUM OF THE DEAD

Book 3 of The Papyrus Trilogy

Zoran Živković

Translated from the Serbian
by

Vuk Tošić

Cadmus Press
2017

Contents

It was just past nine as I drew up in front of the entrance to the City Cemeteries Administration Building. I had not expected to find a free space so easily. Having passed from time to time, I remembered that it was rather busy with people trying to park their cars nearby. The rush was understandable bearing in mind that on average around a hundred people died every day in the city, and that in the majority of cases funerals were scheduled here. However, it seemed too early still for the business of death.

The squat bungalow was surrounded by a narrow garden full of well-tended greenery, and separated from the street by a cast-iron fence. The old-fashioned building was likely a private villa originally. Its façade did not provide any hint as to which department was housed there. The mosaic of bright yellow and red bricks and the tall windows would have better suited the services related to entrance into the world, rather than departure from it.

As I got out of my car, it occurred to me that I had never set foot in this house, even though death was an integral part of my job as an inspector. There had not yet been any reason for me to come. Now there was a reason, although I had not quite understood what was the matter. It was also unclear to my colleague Bumbaković, who had called me from the switchboard just as I was headed towards my office at the Police Headquarters, twenty minutes earlier.

"You should go over to the City Cemeteries Administration, on. . . ."

"I know where it is," I said, interrupting him. "What's happened?"

There was a short pause.

"I'm not sure. The woman who called was excited and mixed up. She said something about some books. . . .that they were amiss. . . ."

I sighed. Why did everyone on the police force immediately think of me the minute anybody mentioned books?

"If it isn't anything more serious than something being wrong with some books, just send the nearest patrol. Let them see what exactly it's about. The City Cemeteries Administration isn't on my way. It might take me as much as half an hour to get there in this traffic."

There was another pause. Bumbaković coughed before continuing.

"I would have sent a patrol already, but the woman asked for you specifically."

"Me?" I asked, slowing down a bit. "Why?"

"I didn't understand that either. Do you want me to play back the recording of our conversation?"

"There's no need. I'm on my way."

I returned my cell phone to my jacket pocket and stepped on the gas.

I HAD TO PUSH quite hard in order to budge the gate in the cast-iron fence. The short gravel path led up to three wide steps at the entrance to the former villa. The doors were tall, as were the windows. Above the upper left corner a small camera blended into the yellow brick background like a chameleon.

I reached for the door handle, but someone on the inside beat me to it. The door opened towards me halfway and the space was filled by the figure of a short, bald, stumpy man with watery eyes. He looked like he was well into his fifties. His dark blue guard's uniform was rather wrinkled. Blinking, he began speaking rapidly before I had even had a chance to introduce myself.

"I didn't close an eye all night, I swear. They just keep on accusing me of sleeping on the job. And that I drink. No one came in. You can check the recording." He glanced up towards the camera. "It's all a frame-up, so I. . . ."

"Mr. Rabrenović!" A sharp female voice from within interrupted him.

Flinching as though caught in the act, he hastily opened the door wide, and scampered into his glass booth across from the entrance.

The broad corridor was covered with thick red and yellow carpeting. A tall woman dressed in a dark gray suit and a lighter blouse of the same color approached me from the left. She was closer to fifty than forty. Her shoulder-length dark hair, with ends curling toward her chin, framed her long sunken face. Large glasses hung on a dark cord around her neck, resting on a mere hint of a bosom. She wore almost no makeup, and had on low-heeled shoes.

She raised her eyebrows slightly as she stood in front of me.

"Inspector Lukić?" Her voice had become softer, but was still brusque.

"Dejan Lukić," I responded with a nod, holding out my hand. "Good morning."

Before accepting it, she sized me up me once more, as though in slight disbelief; she must have imagined police inspectors differently. Her grip was firm.

"Good morning. Hristina Leleković, Head of the City Cemeteries Administration. We have been waiting for you, Inspector. The police should arrive faster in such extraordinary cases."

"The police are always fast, except when a specific inspector is requested. Then it inevitably takes a little time."

"Well, let's not go into that now. Before we proceed

any further, I have to tell you that your investigation must not jeopardize the normal functioning of our service. Any interruption or obstruction is out of the question. The City Cemeteries Administration does not suspend its operations even in times of war. Other affairs can be postponed, but not burials. Nothing is more important. I hope this is clear to you."

"Absolutely. However, I still don't know what I'm supposed to be investigating."

"Didn't your colleague inform you? I explained everything to him clearly."

"From what he conveyed to me, I only understood that something unusual had happened, involving some books. Could you please explain it to me too?"

She sighed, shook her head, and motioned me towards the stairs next to the guard's booth. "Please follow me," she said as she passed me by. I thought she would be taking me upstairs, but instead she headed into the basement.

The downstairs corridor was covered with the same red and yellow carpeting, but it seemed shabbier, perhaps because of the slightly weaker lighting. We headed right. Large black and white photos of cemeteries hung on the walls between the office doors. The inscriptions on the plates beneath the black frames were too small to read in passing.

The administrator stopped in front of the last door on the left. Before knocking, she glanced past me down the corridor. As though waiting right inside the door, someone instantly unlocked and opened it.

A thin middle-aged man, slightly hunchbacked, moved aside to let us enter, then closed and locked the door again. He wore a dark suit and vest with a gray striped tie. He had a high forehead, thick sideburns and glasses with round metal frames. Without saying a word, he walked to the large desk in the middle of the room and remained standing next to the chair.

I looked around the room. Even though it was not small, it seemed cramped because the walls were covered with bookcases filled with large volumes of equal height and thickness. They were almost the identical dark gray color as the administrator's suit. Walking up the gravel path I had noticed barred basement windows along the entire width of the building. They were not visible here, which meant that the bookcases covered them. Someone considered storing books to be more important than daylight. The only lighting in the room was provided by a square ceiling light.

A large volume lay open on the desk, and alongside it a bundle of documents. In front of the book was something that I hadn't seen in a long time—an inkwell. The bottle stood on a black metal stand with arched supports, the pen shaft sticking out. A round vase with a single yellow flower had been placed behind the writing set.

The administrator moved away from the door a little and gestured vaguely to the bookcases.

"This is perhaps the most important office in our Administration. The Archive. And this is precisely where someone chose to harm us."

"Are the archives still kept the old-fashioned way?" I asked. "I thought that all departments had gone digital long ago."

"This one has too, of course. Modernization cannot be avoided, although our experiences with it have been rather traumatic. On two occasions we almost lost our entire database. Computers might speed things up, but they are not at all as reliable as is generally believed. Can you imagine what a disaster it would be if we were to lose what is kept here?"

She looked at me questioningly, as though expecting me to answer, but as I did not say anything, she continued.

"We keep the only trace that most people even existed—information on where and when they were buried. Everything else has been forgotten, lost. As though they had never even lived. We cannot surrender such a treasure to the imperfections of digital storage alone. That is why, in addition to computer archiving, we have also resorted to the old-fashioned system. We keep records of burials as has been done since ancient times. Here it cannot happen that someone mistakenly or intentionally presses a few keys on the keyboard—and destroys everything. The dead are safe this way."

"It seems that in fact they are not. Why else would you have called the police? What happened?"

The administrator looked briefly at the clerk before answering. Her voice became more subdued.

"Last night someone broke in here and scoured through the books. We discovered it this morning."

"Scoured?"

"Moved them. As you will see, the books are arranged neatly. By number. In the first bookcase," she pointed at the first bookcase on the wall across from the door, "we discovered as many as seven volumes in the wrong place."

I walked up to the bookcase and looked it over from top to bottom. There were twelve books in each of the five rows. The only inscription on the spines was a gold-embossed Arabic numeral at the bottom. The volumes were moved around in all the rows, at first glance—randomly. I tried to open the glass doors, but they were locked.

"Who has the keys to this room and the bookcases?" I asked.

"Only Mr. Trpimirović, the archivist." She turned her head toward the clerk for a moment. "No one else has access here."

"Is there a spare key? With the guard, for example?"

"There are no spares. And even if there were—the guard would certainly not have them." She just waved me away, without adding anything, as though every-thing was clear.

"These are not exactly locks used to protect trea-sures," I said, pointing at the door and the first book-case. "Anyone with any skill at all could open them even without a key."

"They were quite all right until now. Nothing like this has ever happened before. At least, not in the twelve and a half years that I have been administrator." She sighed. "All right, we'll change them. We'll install better ones. We cannot allow this to happen again."

"You should probably upgrade this old-fashioned ar-chive a bit. Install video surveillance. Cameras would be more useful here than in front of the entrance. Had you had them, we would have identified instantly the prankster who decided to play a joke on you."

"Prankster?" she said, the pitch of her voice rising. "This is no prank. It must be taken quite seriously. . . ."

"As far as I can see, no harm has been done. Noth-ing was stolen or destroyed. Several volumes were just moved. Return them to their places—and everything will be as it was. There is no work here for the police."

"I insist that you conduct an investigation. You have to determine who did this."

Now I sighed. First she had made me come over in the worst morning rush-hour traffic, and now she was insisting that I carry out an investigation into someone's juvenile behavior. That is not how you treat a police in-spector, no matter how important all this seemed to her.

I walked up to the desk, slightly raised the volume that lay open and read the number on the spine: 3584.

"Perhaps you wouldn't like what an investigation could uncover."

"What do you mean?"

"You see, in investigations we rely on one rule, which has almost no exceptions: the simplest solution is the most likely one. We can imagine that behind all this is someone from the outside, who crept into the building in the dead of night, past the sleeping or intoxicated guard, while remaining invisible to the video surveillance; or that it was someone on the inside who is adept at burglary. However, why should we resort to such complex explanations when we have at our disposal a significantly simpler one?"

"A simpler one?" she repeated questioningly.

"Yes. There is someone who could very easily pull this off without any nighttime sneaking around and breaking in; someone who could have unlocked both the door and the bookcase without any difficulty, because he is the only one who has the keys to them."

It took her several moments to understand who I was talking about. She opened her mouth to protest, but I beat her to the punch by turning to the archivist.

"Mr. Trpimirović, you discovered that the books had been moved, right?"

"Yes," he answered evenly.

"How did that happen? What led you to pay attention precisely to the first bookcase? The volume that you are working on was not in it. Judging by the number, it is from a completely different part of the room. And if you were not standing in front of the bookcase and staring right at it, you could not have noticed that the books had been rearranged."

For a moment we fell into silence. The administrator's gaze slipped from me to the archivist. His face remained expressionless. He cleared his throat before finally speaking.

"I would like to ask you something, Inspector Lukić."

"How do you know my name? The administrator did not introduce me."

"No, she didn't. But she insisted that you come in particular. And since we waited for a long time for the police to arrive, then it had to be you. What do you think, why did she ask specifically for you?"

I shrugged. "I have no idea. I was leaving that question for the end. I am very interested in why out of all the inspectors she chose me."

"You will get your answer right away."

He leaned over, opened a drawer on the left side of the desk and took out a large yellow envelope. It contained something firm, with a regular shape. He approached the first bookcase, removed a small bunch of keys from his jacket pocket, searched through them briefly, set one aside, and unlocked the glass door. He placed the envelope upright in front of the books in the middle row, then closed the door, without locking it. He left the key in the lock.

"This is how I found it when I came in at eight o'clock. Is it conspicuous enough to attract your attention?"

The yellow rectangle stood out prominently on the dark gray background. One could not overlook it if one's gaze were to rest there for even a brief moment.

"What is it?" I asked, realizing that same instant what a stupid question it was.

A smile passed across the archivist's lips.

"An envelope," he answered matter-of-factly, just as my question merited. He opened the bookcase again and took it out; he then closed and locked the door, and returned the bunch of keys to his pocket. He came up to me and handed me the envelope. "It is addressed to you. That is why we asked for you specifically."

I hesitated a little before accepting it. I turned it right-side up and was presented with four words written across the middle in red pencil "For Inspector Dejan Lukić." I didn't recognize the handwriting.

My eyes moved from the administrator to the archivist. Then I slowly removed the two brass clips from one end, spread out the stuck edges, and peered into the envelope.

∽ 2 ∽

I REMAINED STARING FOR a moment, then briefly raised my eyes once more to Mrs. Leleković and Mr. Trpimirović. I reached for the thing that was inside, but stopped halfway. I set the envelope down on the desk and took out a pair of plastic gloves from my inside jacket pocket. I put them on hastily and picked up the envelope again.

It took some effort to remove the book whose corners kept getting caught on the plastic lining. Whoever had placed it inside had doubtless had similar difficulties. I put the envelope back on the desk and examined the volume in the palm of my hand. It was approximately a B5 format, rather thick. There was no lettering on the leather cover.

I turned the book over, expecting it to be face down, but there was no inscription on that side either. I looked at the back once again, then at the spine. Nothing interrupted the monotonous whiteness of the cover.

I opened the book and started leafing through it. At first I turned one page at a time, but I quickly realized that there was no reason to make slow progress, so I quickly flipped through to the end. The plastic glove didn't hinder me much in doing this.

Like the cover, the book was also empty. The snow-white surfaces had only the page numbers in the outer corners at the bottom. Printed on the last page before the endpaper was the number 2048. I was convinced that paper that thin was used only for Bibles.

I closed the white book and took a look at the archivist. He looked back at me, still with an expressionless face.

Not knowing about the envelope addressed to me, I had rashly concluded that it was a case with a simple explanation. Whoever had pulled this off, it was not mere juvenile behavior. One does not obtain such

an unusual book and get a specific police inspector involved just to play a prank on the administrator.

"What is it?" Mrs. Leleković broke the silence, while
pointing at the volume in my hand.

"A book," I answered, also matter-of-factly. "Why
didn't you tell me immediately about the envelope?"

"Because it isn't the most important thing," she responded irately. "We are deeply honored that it occurred
to someone to leave packages for you precisely here, but
we are very concerned that this jeopardizes the safety of
our archive. And it worries us even more that you have
no intention of carrying out an investigation."

I sighed again, then said apologetically: "There will
be an investigation, of course."

"Very well," she said with a light nod. "I hope that
you haven't forgotten what I first drew your attention
to: your investigation cannot interfere with the running of our administration."

"There will be no interference. I am just leaving."

I picked up the envelope from the desk. I hesitated
briefly over whether to replace the book inside so that
I could remove the plastic gloves. But that would undoubtedly have taken time.

"But you haven't . . . investigated. . . ." the administrator protested.

"On the contrary. I have seen everything there is to
see. I have even spoken to everyone that I need to speak
to. There is no more work for me here. For now."

"Won't you look for some . . . traces . . . of who
broke in here?"

"It wouldn't do any good. Whoever did this certainly made sure not to leave any traces."

"You can take a look at what the camera in front of
the entrance recorded. . . ."

"There is no need. The guard has already looked at it.
He didn't see anything unusual."

"And you trust him?"

"I have no reason not to trust him. He could have been drunk as a skunk all night, but he was definitely sober when he looked at the recording this morning."

I could see by the administrator's wavering eyes that she was frantically thinking what else she could propose, but nothing was coming to mind. I started towards the door, stopping after two steps. I returned to the desk and looked at the open book. Mr. Trpmirović's handwriting was significantly different from that on the envelope.

"What kind of an investigation will it be, then?" asked the administrator as I started back once more towards the exit. "What will you investigate?"

"The only lead that I have," I answered, rapping the knuckle of my index finger on the white book.

I unlocked the door and went out into the corridor. She joined me hastily. A moment later the door closed, followed right away by the sound of the key turning in the lock.

Halfway to the stairwell I stopped in front of one of the cemetery photos. I drew closer and read the inscription on the brass plate, then looked closely at the picture.

"Nice cemetery," I said after we had continued on.

"The others are also nice." The administrator pointed down the corridor. "Unfortunately most people don't realize that. They stay clear of cemeteries, even though it is only in them that they can find complete tranquility."

"Perhaps that is precisely what puts them off. They lack a little vivaciousness. There will be plenty of time for complete tranquility. . . ."

"Vivaciousness!" the administrator grunted. "Those who care about vivaciousness remain unprepared, and one needs to prepare. . . ."

She left the sentence unfinished because we had reached the ground floor. There were people in the corridor now. The guard's booth was empty.

"We'll stay in touch during the investigation. Please let me know immediately if something out of the ordinary happens. Have you written down my cell phone number?"

I was sure that she would pull out a notepad and pencil from one of her suit pockets, but a cell phone appeared in her hand. She skillfully pressed several buttons and entered the number that I dictated to her.

"Goodbye, Mrs. Leleković." The gloves spared me another handshake with her.

I had half-turned towards the exit when her voice stopped me.

"I have to tell you something, Inspector Lukić. It wasn't at all nice that you suspected Mr. Trpimirović. He is the best clerk in our administration."

"It's his own fault. He should have told me everything immediately, and not put the envelope away in the drawer."

"In any case, you could apologize to him, now that you no longer suspect him."

For a long moment I just looked at her.

"The envelope didn't change anything in that regard. It was still simplest for him to pull it all off."

"But why? What reason would he have to move the books, and then to involve a police inspector as well? That would be quite irrational, and Mr. Trpimirović is the embodiment of rationality."

"Even the most rational people are sometimes led to take unreasonable steps. Perhaps he could no longer take the years of being denied daylight for the sake of storing records of burials. . . ."

Before she had to time to respond, I completed my interrupted movement and left the building of the City Cemeteries Administration.

I was two steps from the gate when my private cell phone rang.

∽ 3 ∾

I STOPPED, TOOK IT out of my inner jacket pocket and looked at the screen: Vera.

"Are you busy?" she asked after I had picked up.

"Not any more. I was just leaving the City Cemeteries Administration."

There was a brief silence. When Vera spoke again her voice had a different tone.

"What are you doing at the City Cemeteries Administration?"

"Someone decided to toy with the necrophiliac administrator. They rearranged the records of the burials in the archives."

"They could have come up with something more original. They were imitating our patients."

"That crossed my mind too. Mrs. Stojanović, right?"

"Yes, poor Mrs. Dragana Stojanović. But we didn't call the police because of her harmless fiddling with the books."

"I gave the administrator a piece of my mind for having to come over here in the rush-hour traffic. It took me almost half an hour."

"Couldn't someone closer have gone?"

I looked down for a moment at the white volume and envelope under my arm.

"As soon as it turned out that it was a problem involving books, anyone else was out of the question."

Vera giggled.

"That's the way it goes when a person has a reputation of being well-read."

I cleared my throat. "What's new with you?"

"I just got an unusual offer."

She stopped, so I asked: "I hope it's not an indecent one."

"No, unfortunately. . . ."

"Unfortunately?"

"Indecent ones are the most profitable. Although this one isn't bad either."

"A decent offer that is not bad?"

"Alright, I won't exactly be fabulously rich, but my overall financial situation will certainly improve if I accept it."

"What could it be?"

"Try to guess. Let's see whether your inspector's insight has improved. You've grown a bit rusty in that department lately."

I pondered for a moment.

"You have been offered to write a book entitled *How I Seduced an Uninsightful Police Inspector*?"

"I seduced you? The inspector isn't only uninsightful but his memory is also failing. Not to mention how indecent that book would be."

I had to move to the side of the path to let pass five or six people, who had gathered in front of the gate while I was standing there. Suddenly it was like someone had fired a gun that only they had heard, and the race was on. They rushed into the yard, almost running the short distance to the entrance. I looked at my watch: 09:30. The business of death had started.

"Alright, the dimwitted and senile inspector gives up," I said while walking out into the street, after the last person in the group had passed. "What kind of an offer did you get?"

"To sell the inventory and books from the Papyrus." Vera's voice had become serious.

"To whom?"

"I don't know. I got a call from the Samardžić Law Offices. They represent the buyer, who wants to remain anonymous. They only hinted that it was a wealthy collector."

"They really offered you a good price?"

Vera was silent for a few moments, then told me the amount in a muted voice. I whistled in awe.

"That's a lot more than the inventory and books are worth, right?"

"At least fifty times more than the market value."

"Why would he offer you so much?"

"He obviously cares strongly about including what remains of the Papyrus in his collection."

"What collection? What is it that this anonymous wealthy collector collects?"

"I have no idea. I recently read a book about out-landish collectors. You'd never guess what all they collect. . . ."

"Still, fifty times more. . . ."

"Things don't have just a market value. The Papyrus was certainly not an ordinary bookstore. That is how much the books and inventory from it are worth to the collector. Who knows, perhaps he is counting on them being worth even more in the future, and he sees this as a good investment."

"How much is what you kept of the Papyrus worth to you?"

Vera didn't answer right away. Her voice again grew soft when she continued.

"I would never sell it at market price."

"And for a price fifty times as much?" I asked, also quietly.

"I don't know," she answered, after a fresh hesitation. "I would have to think about it. Unfortunately I don't have much time. The offer stands only until eleven o'clock."

"Today?"

"Today, yes. I have to make a decision in the next hour and a half."

"Why in such a short time?"

"I didn't get an explanation for that either. The law office believes that the syntagma 'wealthy eccentric collector' is a sufficient answer to all my questions."

I sighed. "That's tough."

"It is. What do you think, what should I do?"

Now it was my turn to pause.

"I don't know, but whatever you choose—I will support you."

"You're not of much help in making decisions, but it still feels good."

"Did you expect more from an uninsightful inspector?"

"I didn't, but I still love him."

"I love you too. Let me know when you reach a decision."

"No one will know before you."

I returned the telephone to my jacket pocket and took out my car key. I placed the envelope on the passenger seat, removed the plastic gloves and laid them over the white book. I still hadn't pulled the car out completely when I heard the angry honking of two competitors for the empty parking space right in front of the entrance to the City Cemeteries Administration.

∽ 4 ∽

AFTER PARKING THE CAR in the underground garage at the Police Headquarters, I first put on the plastic gloves again, then took the envelope and the book. I did not go immediately to my office on the fifth floor, but rather towards the entrance to the basement area, near the elevator. A corridor illuminated by neon lights extended beyond the metal door. It was here that all the technical services were located, with the exception of the Communications Department, which was on the seventh floor.

Walking towards the opposite end of the corridor, I greeted two colleagues in passing. The last door on the right had a sign with the legend "Laboratory." I knocked and entered.

Workstations with a number of apparatus were arranged along the walls of the room. Some were working, and one made a muffled humming sound. The upper space contained several metal shelves with glass dishes of various sizes and shapes, plastic containers, tubes, measurement instruments, utensils, and the occasional book or folder. The whiteboard across from the door was partially filled with chemical symbols. A slender vase with several yellow flowers stood in the right rear corner, in contrast with everything else.

The central part of the room was filled by a spacious rectangular table. It was covered with laboratory equipment, as well as two large computer monitors.

"Hello, Ms. Mirković," I said to the girl in a white lab coat sitting on the left-hand side of the table. She was using an instrument that looked like a microscope with two eyepieces. There was no on else in the lab.

ANA MIRKOVIĆ HAD BEEN hired by the police department a few months earlier, straight out of school. She was short, round, with cropped brown hair and high-set cheeks. She kept to herself, and seemed skilled despite her young age. We had collaborated on several occasions and every time she'd exceeded my expectations. The praise I gave her appeared to cause problems for her.

Our relationship strayed beyond the professional on only one occasion. Our last conversation had not ended with her wordless, bashful smile, which was how she usually responded to my praise. She just looked at me without any expression for several moments, then with a hint of reluctance she asked me an unexpected question.

"Could you recommend a good novel?"

I sighed. Police officers are no less prone to gossip than the rest of the world. Quite the opposite. Who knows what they had told this innocent girl about me.

"It would be my pleasure," I responded. "However,

I don't know anything about your literary taste. What topics appeal to you?"

"Death," said Ms. Mirković without hesitation.

"Death?" I repeated in disbelief.

Seeing my expression made her smile widely for the first time.

"Death that is told as comedy," she quickly added, as though wanting to justify herself.

"Ah, so . . . That's better," I said, also with a smile.

We were silent for a moment while I searched my memory. She waited patiently, with her eyes fixed on me.

"Have you read anything by Saramago?" I finally asked.

She shook her head. "I haven't, but I've been planning to."

"Excellent. Then first take his novel *Death with Interruptions*. I think that it will suit you."

"Is it funny?"

"Irresistibly."

She nodded. "Thank you for the recommendation."

It had been about three weeks since that chat. We had not worked together in the meantime, but we did meet several times in passing and exchanged a few words. However, she had not mentioned the book at all. Perhaps she still had not read it, or perhaps she did not find Saramago's dark humor amusing, but didn't feel comfortable saying so.

"Hello, Inspector Lukić," she responded with a smile, looking up from the eyepieces.

"Everyone has deserted you?" I pointed to the empty seats at the table.

"That's my karma."

I looked at her suspiciously. "You don't expect me to believe that, do you?"

"Believe it or don't. Alright, they also leave for other

reasons, not only to desert me. It's like everyone is just waiting for an excuse to go somewhere outside, or at least where there are windows. They feel claustrophobic here."

"And you?"

"I don't mind the underworld, at least not yet, but I've only been here a short while. Perhaps I will start to feel stifled here after a bit as well."

"And perhaps the laboratory and other technical services will be relocated somewhere higher up. There has been talk of it."

"So I've heard. My colleague who has been here the longest says that there was also talk about it thirty years ago, when he first arrived."

"I don't think you will have to wait that long."

She smiled again. "You've comforted me. What can I do for you, Inspector?"

I approached and handed her the envelope and the book.

"Would you be so kind as to check this for fingerprints? There's no hurry. Finish what you are doing first."

"That isn't urgent either. I'll check right away. Besides, I am in your debt."

She removed a pair of plastic gloves from a drawer, put them on and took the envelope and the book. She kept them in her hands.

"In my debt?" I asked, as I took off the gloves.

"Saramago, remember?"

"Ah, that. I was just wondering whether you had had the opportunity to read the funny novel about death."

"I read it over the first weekend after you had recommended it."

"I hope it didn't disappoint you."

"On the contrary, it captivated me. I occasionally laughed out loud."

"It's Saramago's unique skill, laughter that stems

from the morbid. It is even more prominent in *Blindness*."

"Thank you for the new recommendation. However, there is something in *Death with Interruptions* that scared me."

"Was there? What was it?"

"The idea that there is no more death."

"That scared you?" I asked in puzzlement.

"Very much. I once even dreamed that I found myself in such a world. I woke up terrified."

"What is so terrifying about that? Wouldn't you like never to die?"

The girl looked at me piercingly for a moment before shaking her head.

"It isn't about dying but about growing old. Imagine getting older and older, and there being no death to put an end to that agony."

"That never occurred to me. All right, perhaps the world without death would also be a world without aging."

"You have consoled me yet again, Inspector." She nodded towards the envelope and the book. "This will be done quickly. Should I bring the items and the report to your office?"

"I would appreciate it. It would also give you reason to leave the underworld for a little while."

∽ 5 ∾

Ms. Mirković knocked on the door of my office about twenty minutes later. She entered, approached the desk I was seated at, and placed on its edge the envelope, the book and two pieces of paper.

"There wasn't much work, Inspector. I found fingerprints only on the envelope. In addition to yours, just one other person touched it with their bare hands."

She picked up the top piece of paper, which contained her report, then rapped the knuckle of her index finger on the black-and-white photo that took up a quarter of the bottom piece of paper. The archivist from the City Cemeteries Administration looked several years younger in the picture.

"A certain Tihomir Trpimirović. I barely found anything on him. An impeccable citizen, one might say. We don't have any information about him in the database. He has actually never had any dealings with the police. This is from the general birth records. Even there he appears quite inconspicuous. He has lived at the same address since birth, single, no children, just one job—at the City Cemeteries Administration." She stopped and smiled. "It is as though he stepped out of *Death with Interruptions*."

I responded with a smile of my own. "Reality and literature have more in common than is believed."

Watching me carefully, she waited for me to say something more, but since I did not, a shadow of disappointment passed over her face as she continued.

"I also googled him. There is no mention of him. Not a single hit. As though he doesn't even exist. Being so digitally inconspicuous is extremely rare."

"It doesn't surprise me. I met with him this morning. Computers have been banned from his workplace. He uses a nib pen and inkwell. Apparently that is what he is like privately too."

"Not everyone lives in their own era," she said with a shrug.

"In any case, thank you for your efforts. You have done an excellent job once again."

She gave me her usual bashful smile, but didn't walk away as on previous occasions.

"Regarding the book. . . ." she said and then stopped.

"Yes?"

"It has absolutely no fingerprints. Albeit, that is how most books are when they come off the printing press.

Machines have been doing all the work at printing houses for some time now. Copies don't pass though human hands at all. However, someone had to place this one in the envelope. Machines still don't do that. If it was Mr. Trpimirović, why did he avoid leaving prints on the book, but didn't care about leaving them on the envelope?"

It was I who shrugged now. "I have no idea."

"And there is the book itself. I have never heard of one that has no lettering. Even if this weren't a book at all, but for example a luxurious diary or notebook, there would be some writing, right?"

"I guess."

"Someone sent it to you?"

"Obviously." I pointed towards the envelope.

"You weren't expecting it?"

"No, I wasn't."

I saw in her sparkling eyes that she wanted to continue asking questions in this direction, but she was discouraged by the brevity of my answers. It was clear to her that I did not wish to discuss it.

We were silent for a while.

"Just one more thing. That paper. . . ."

"Paper?"

"It's strange. . . ."

"In what sense?"

"I don't know . . . I'd like to test it. I was rushing to finish the fingerprint analysis, and there wasn't time to look into it. Would you give me the book again? I'll keep it for no more than half an hour."

"How about I bring it to you in half an hour? I'd like to look at it a bit first. I haven't had an opportunity yet."

She nodded. "Of course, Inspector. I'll be in the lab."

"Ms. Mirković," I said, stopping her after she had already opened the door.

She turned around and looked at me inquisitively.

"I hope that *Blindness* will not frighten you like *Death with Interruptions*. It's not as funny, and it is more morbid."

She smiled. "It isn't easy to frighten me twice. Not even Saramago could manage that."

I went to reach for the book when the girl had left, but my action remained incomplete. My private cell phone rang from my inner jacket pocket.

"Do you have a little time?" Vera asked.

"A lot, if needed."

"A little will be enough. I've reached a decision."

"You'll sell the Papyrus inventory."

"How did you guess?"

"It wasn't a guess. I relied on my famous inspector's insightfulness."

Vera laughed. "Just don't become arrogant. It didn't exactly require any special insightfulness."

"It didn't," I agreed.

"It doesn't make any sense to keep the remains of the Papyrus. I will never go back to that business. That is quite certain now. Those things are just a painful memory. Not to mention the rent for the storage unit where I keep them. That is a significant expense for an unemployed former bookstore keeper."

"The unemployed former bookstore keeper will now become nearly a fat cat. A pitiful police inspector will hardly be a match for her any longer."

"Well, my dear pitiful police inspector, work on your insightfulness, and perhaps you will earn a promotion and greater benefits. Just hurry up—it is a known fact that wealthy bachelorettes are besieged by suitors. . . ."

"Does that mean that the wealthy bachelorette will not be engaging in anything other than choosing the best suitor? I can hardly imagine you as such an easy-going person."

"Oh, no, the suitors will only be my hobby. Wealth will finally allow me to do what I've always dreamt of."

"And that is. . . .?"

"I won't tell you just yet. Not to jinx it. Wait until I actually become wealthy first. I've told the law office about my decision. We will meet there at half past eleven to sign the contract. Everything should be over by noon. They will pay me the money as soon as I hand over the keys to the storage unit."

"Why are they in such a hurry?" I asked, after a short hesitation.

"You know their wild card answer—'the wealthy eccentric collector.' Well, now I'm in a hurry too. I need to get ready and get across town. I'm already running late. Kisses."

She hung up before I had time to say "Kisses to you too."

∽ 6 ∾

I PICKED UP THE book and stared at it in my open left hand. There was something sensual in the touch of the leather cover. I had not experienced it holding the white volume while wearing gloves. Previously it had only been an object, and now for an instant I had the deceptive impression that something living was in the palm of my hand.

I opened the book and flipped through several pages. I then took one between my thumb and index finger and rubbed it slightly, the better to feel its texture. Nothing seemed unusual. What did Ms. Mirković mean when she said that the paper seemed strange?

I raised the book towards the window, without letting go of the page. The thin paper became semitransparent under the strong daylight. The shadow of my index finger was clearly visible from the other side. I put the book down and leafed through it again. The quick succession of more than two thousand empty pages flipped past my eyes.

I shut the book and then examined the thick volume from all sides some more. However, there was nothing to see. The only obvious thing was that such a book had to be expensive even without being printed, especially since it existed in only one copy. This was what made it stand out, that and the way it had been delivered to me. What I usually got was significantly cheaper and reached me by simpler means.

It was inevitable that I would be marked out by the role that I'd played in the cases of the "Last Book" and the "Grand Manuscript." The full contingent of weirdoes, paranoids and conspiracy theorists saw me as the person with whom they had to get in contact right away. They had to inform me of the discoveries they had made, and which mainly concerned the fate of the world.

I usually received the messages by email. They somehow found my address. When the number of emails exceeded ten per day I changed my address, but the lull was short-lived. They would find the new one too, and the torrent of messages continued unabated. I changed addresses three more times, and then I finally gave up. I didn't pay attention to such emails any more. I simply deleted them. The record was a hundred and thirty-seven deleted messages, which is how many had accumulated between two Saturdays.

While deleting them, now and then I would read the beginning of an email, and sometimes even a longer passage. Occasionally I would laugh heartily at the incredible ideas these people had come up with, and I was tempted several times to propose that they try to turn them into prose. They would make excellent detective novels.

I also received letters in envelopes, as well as packages, although not as often. The senders preferred to leave them personally in my mailbox, convinced that email and postal communication were being monitored. The messages were no different from those in the emails, and the packages mainly contained books. They were mostly amateur and self-published, but I also received official publications, with an appropriate short or longer text on how one should read them in order to uncover their hidden meaning. These books even included several great works of world literature.

Occasionally I received publications with jackets that didn't belong to them. The work would have its own title, while the added jacket would have the inscription *The Last Book* or *The Grand Manuscript*. On one occasion someone wanted to be funny and put *The First Book* and *The Minor Manuscript* on the jackets. I threw away the letters, as I did the emails, but I kept the books. In time a rather large collection of these works accumulated, and it eventually got its own bookshelf.

It was most uncommon for them to call me on the phone. They would get in touch with me through the police switchboard, and only once did someone get hold of my work cell phone number. The calls did not last long. All it took for them to hang up was for me to tell them the number from which they were calling. I imagine this left a particular impression on those who believed that they were invisible if they switched off the caller identification.

This morning's attempt to get me involved in some weird business was the most complex one so far. Not only was the person behind everything willing to go to considerable expense for what they had set out to do, but they had also pulled it off very skillfully. My main suspect was still Mr. Trpimirović, but I didn't have any evidence that would incriminate him.

If it really was him, he'd made sure not to overlook any of the details that amateurs always miss. He hadn't left any fingerprints on or in the book, and he'd found someone with different handwriting to write the four words on the envelope. I picked it up off the desk and looked at the red lettering. The letters were round and upright, unlike the archivist's elongated and slanted script in the burial records.

Well, he was doing well so far. Nevertheless, we'd see how he would do next time. And there would certainly be a next time. One does not invest this much in a single performance—where among other things the police inspector is being pulled by the nose—only to end it with the volumes that were moved around in the underground bookcase being put back in their places and me adding another book to my odd collection. The main event was yet to come.

I had just placed the envelope back on my desk when my work cell phone rang.

"Inspector Lukić," my colleague Bumbaković called from the switchboard. "You are being requested by the National Library."

"I'm in my office. Patch them through to my landline."

"All right."

I picked up the receiver as soon as it rang.

"Inspector Dejan Lukić."

"Inspector, you have to come to the National Library immediately." The young female voice sounded rather excited.

"To whom am I speaking?"

"Please forgive me. I didn't introduce myself. It's because I'm excited. Olivera Šuvaković. Deputy Head of the Department of Old and Rare Books."

"Pleased to make your acquaintance, Mrs. Šuvaković."

"Miss. . . ."

"Miss. What has happened?"

There was a moment of silence.

"I can't tell you, Inspector. I mean, not over the phone . . . Only when you get here. . . ."

"Has someone . . . been injured?"

"Oh, no, worse than that. . . ."

"Killed?"

"No, no, even worse, I tell you."

What could be worse than that? Nonetheless, there was no sense in asking Miss Šuvaković, who was obviously beside herself. Arguing with her would only be a waste of time.

"I'll send the nearest patrol immediately."

"No! You have to come personally! It concerns you too. . . ."

I fell silent for a moment.

"I'll come right away."

"Inspector!" she shouted. "Don't use the main entrance, please! We have to be discreet. It's very important. I'll wait for you by the staff entrance. In the rear of the National Library building. Do you know where it is?"

"I'll find it, don't worry. I'll see you in about fifteen minutes."

I hung up the receiver and hurried towards the door. Going around the desk I grabbed the book. It would take only a minute to drop it off at the lab.

I almost ran down the basement corridor, and entered without knocking. Mr. Grubijanić, the head of the laboratory, was the only person seated at the large table.

"Ms. Mirković isn't here?" I asked, pointing towards the place where she had been sitting.

"She wasn't here when I came in a little while ago. She must have popped out. Should I call her?"

He reached for the upper pocket of his white lab coat and pulled out his cell phone.

"No, thank you. It's not urgent. I'll leave this for her. I saw her earlier. She knows what to do."

I walked up to the left-hand side of the table and placed the white book next to the instrument with two eyepieces. Then I hurried to the garage.

～ 7 ～

I HAD TO SHOW the guard my badge for him to let me into the small parking lot behind the National Library building. Of the forty or so spaces only two were unoccupied. As I approached the staff entrance I saw a female figure standing behind the glass doors. She was of average height, slightly portly, with long red hair, wearing a dark red suit and a beige blouse. She was still in her thirties.

She opened the door when I was two steps away from it.

"Mr. Lukić?"

"Dejan Lukić." I held out my hand. "Hello, Miss Šuvaković."

"Hello," she responded in a rush.

She pulled my hand slightly as we shook, as though she wanted me to enter as soon as possible.

"This way, please."

She pointed towards the elevator opposite the door. As we quickly crossed the lobby, she glanced to the right. An older lady in a light-gray uniform watched us curiously from the reception desk.

As we waited for the elevator, Miss Šuvaković played nervously with a small bunch of keys. She kept her head down, staring at the floor in front of her, obviously avoiding conversation. I was silent too.

As soon as we entered the elevator she separated one of the keys in the bunch. She placed it in the opening at the bottom of a vertical series of small square numbered boxes, and turned it a quarter-turn clockwise. There was no inscription next to the keyhole, and above it was "–3."

"We're going down deep," I said with a smile as the elevator started to move, just to dispel the silence.

"The greatest treasures are always the deepest." She tried to return the smile, but it came out as a grimace.

When the elevator doors opened, there was no corridor in front of us. It gave straight onto our destination. There was no need for an ante-room because one could only get there by using the elevator key. This was also the key to the Department of Old and Rare Books.

The room was about fifteen meters long and five meters wide, but it seemed cramped because of the low ceiling. There were only slightly more than two meters separating it from the floor. And just as at the City Cemeteries Administration, the walls were covered in bookcases. However, these were not mere storage for uniform volumes, but genuine works of art. The hand-carved walnut must have been extremely costly, but nothing cheaper would have been fitting for these books.

The conditions in the room were also in keeping with their preservation. The temperature was slightly lower than regular room temperature, and the humidity had been completely removed, although the dry air did not seem stale. Wide lights along the spine and edge of the vault cast a soft bluish light.

As I stepped inside I looked behind me. The view of the exceptional books and shelves was not spoiled by regular metal elevator doors. They too were lined with walnut on the interior.

Along every wall a brass ladder on guide rails extended the entire height, even though a person slightly taller than average could easily have reached the top row of books without their aid.

There were five horizontal hand-carved bookcases in the center of the room, resembling pool tables. The upper portions were made of glass, which allowed only visual access to the most valuable and sensitive editions beneath.

The sixth element in the row, nearest to the door, was a massive desk. It was surrounded by eight chairs, and on it were as many desk lamps. The center of the desk was given over to flowers. In a shallow porcelain flowerpot there grew a low green bush with a sprinkling of small yellow blooms. These plants obviously didn't mind the absence of sunlight deep underground.

At first glance it seemed to me that there was no one in the great hall, but then a small figure emerged from behind a green screen and walked towards us. The woman was barely one meter sixty tall. She was already nearing retirement age, with short dark hair, a suit and a slightly lighter turtleneck, whose exact color was difficult to make out in this lighting. She wore a large oval brooch on her left shoulder.

Miss Šuvaković stepped aside and waited for the older woman to approach.

"Mrs. Evgenija Ognjanović, Administrator of the Department of Old and Rare Books," she said, introducing her. "Inspector Dejan Lukić."

"Pleased to meet you," I said, holding out my hand. She held it slightly longer than necessary in a soft grip, sizing me up, although not in the same way that Mrs. Leleković had done. Her eyes were not filled with distrust or reproach, but rather curiosity and relief.

"Dear Inspector, thank you for coming so quickly. Olivera and I are completely beside ourselves. We have no idea what to do."

"It is extremely important that you understand," the deputy intruded before the administrator had the opportunity to continue, "that this must remain in the strictest confidence. No one besides the three of us can know what has happened. There would be immeasurable consequences if word got out. Immeasurable . . . You have to promise not to say a word to anyone."

"I cannot promise anything until I know what has happened. You indicated that it is something worse than violent death, and that can hardly be kept secret. I can only promise that I will be very discreet."

Miss Šuvaković had already opened her mouth to say

something, but Mrs. Ognjanović interrupted her with a raised hand.

"You must forgive Olivera, Inspector. She was very wound up when she said that. Of course, that is not what she meant. All this has been a great blow to her; to me too, after all. Both of us are very concerned with the reputation of our department. I have spent decades building it up, and she will soon take over, since I am retiring. This is the first time that this reputation has been seriously compromised."

I glanced over the lavish shelves full of even more lavish books.

"It is difficult for me to imagine what could compromise the reputation of this place. Perhaps something has been stolen, despite all the security measures?"

The two women exchanged glances, and then the administrator coughed lightly.

"Precisely the opposite, Inspector," she said in a somewhat softer voice.

"The opposite?" I repeated in confusion.

"Something has been brought in that has no right to be here."

I stared at her, expecting her to continue, but she fell quiet. We passed several moments in silence.

"I'll show you right away," she said finally, "but first I have to prepare you. Olivera said that this also concerns you. Do you recall?"

"How could I forget?"

"It wasn't only one . . . thing . . . that was brought in, but rather two. The second is addressed to you."

Now she stared at me, waiting for me to respond, but I remained mute.

"Come!" she said, again speaking first, and took me around the large desk.

The part concealed by the plants was not empty. There was something covered with a large white scarf-like cloth, between the two central lamps. Mrs. Ognjanović glanced at me, then pulled away the cover with one swift movement, as though performing a magic trick.

∽ 8 ∽

My eyes first came to rest on the larger and more prominent of the two objects that had been under the scarf. The yellow envelope seemed to be the same as the one at the City Cemeteries Administration archive. Judging by the silhouetted contours, it too contained a book. Even the red inscription was no different: the same four words, the same rounded upright script.

I was aware that the two women were gauging me, but I disappointed their expectations and again remained silent. I only approached the desk to get a better view of the second object. As I leaned over the small, but very thick antique book with a dark red cover, a shout rang out behind me.

"Don't touch anything!"

I straightened up and briefly turned to Miss Šuvaković. "I had no intention of doing so."

Placing my hands behind my back, I returned to my observation of the book and tried to make out the title, albeit in vain. What was once an inscription could only be made out by the remaining specks of unpeeled gold embossing. The shapes of two letters that were only slightly more visible led me to the conclusion that the title might be in Gothic script.

This time I turned to the administrator and looked at her inquiringly.

"*Das Buch der Auferstehung,*" she replied to my unspoken question.

"*The Book of Resurrection,*" I heard from behind my back.

"Danke," I responded, without turning around.

"Anonymous author," Mrs. Ognjanović continued. "Printed in Mainz in 1488."

"An incunabulum," I muttered to myself.

"That's right. And a very special one at that. This is the first banned printed book. It's no surprise. Over more than seven hundred pages the unknown author provides short entries about people who he believes deserve above all to be resurrected after the Second Coming of Christ. These are primarily historical persons, but there are also those who were the author's living contemporaries. Trouble occurred when it came to the living contemporaries whom he left out. He was convinced that those who were included would offer sufficient protection, but it turned out that a wounded vanity was much stronger than a satisfied one. Those who had been left out made sure that the book was banned. They did not discover who the author was, so they couldn't burn him at the stake, but they destroyed all the copies they could get their hands on. As far as we know, only one copy remains."

I nodded towards the desk in front of me. "This one?"

She shook her head. "The only copy of *The Book of Resurrection* officially in existence still belongs to one of the most reputable collectors of old books. I've checked. It wasn't easy to pull it off. I couldn't call him and simply ask whether someone had stolen the crown jewel of his collection. I actually had to put on a little performance. Luckily, we've known each other for a long time so I didn't make him suspicious."

"So what is this?"

"There is only one possibility: a second copy that somehow escaped being burned in the late fifteenth century."

I bent over again to take a closer look at the book.

"Are you certain that it is . . . an original?"

"Completely. That was the first thing that we checked. We have an excellent laboratory. The verification lasted a good hour and a half. That is why we didn't call you this morning as soon as we found it. We had to be sure that it wasn't a hoax. That was also a possibility. There is great money at stake in this business."

"So where did the second copy come from? You said that only one remains."

"I said—as far as we know. And you never know everything when it comes to old books. It isn't exactly a rarity for a book that no one was expecting to suddenly turn up out of somewhere. Who knows what else remains hidden in private collections and various depositories of antiquities, that no expert has seen yet. Some owners have no idea how rich they are."

I straightened up again and pointed at the two items on the desk.

"How did these get here?"

The administrator and her deputy exchanged glances again.

"If we knew that, Inspector Lukić, we wouldn't have called you," Miss Šuvaković responded. "We thought that you might have some idea." She looked at the envelope.

"Who exactly found these this morning?" I asked, ignoring her remark.

"Olivera did," Mrs. Ognjanović answered. "She comes in first, shortly before nine o'clock."

I stepped back from the desk a little so that I would not have to keep turning my head towards the women, who stood on each side of me.

"You found the book exactly in this place? Beneath the white cover?"

The deputy nodded.

"Did you immediately lift the cover or did you wait for the administrator?"

"I lifted it immediately, but didn't touch anything until the administrator arrived. When we realized what the book in question was, we took it to the laboratory. We did everything in gloves, of course."

"Of course," I repeated, with a smile. "Who did the testing at the lab?"

"The two of us," Mrs. Ognjanović intervened. "That is one of our duties. It isn't very difficult. We have excellent equipment. You place the book in one instrument and it does everything for you. The only thing that remains is to interpret the results properly."

"Did anyone touch the envelope?" I addressed the deputy again.

She glanced at the administrator, then shook her head.

"Who has the key to the elevator that leads to this department?"

"Only the two of us," said Mrs. Ognjanović. "In the morning, when we come in, we each take our key from the library's main safe, and we return them before leaving. No one else is authorized to take them. There is a third key, a spare, in the safe, in case of an emergency."

"There must also be an emergency exit, in addition to the elevator, right?"

The administrator looked at me briefly, without saying a word. "Only the director of the National Library is authorized to give you that information."

"I thought you wanted everything to stay within the smallest circle. . . ."

The mute stare lasted a bit longer this time. It was apparent from her eyes that she was thinking frantically.

"Please believe me when I say that no one uninvited could have come in that way. . . ."

"I believe you," I said with slight hesitation, then raised my head and scanned the low-lying ceiling. "Do you have video surveillance?"

"Of course," the deputy responded.

"Did you check last night's recordings?"

"There was no recording during the night."

"Why not?"

"The system is set up so that the cameras go on only when something moves in the room. Since nothing moved, nothing was recorded."

"And yesterday's footage? Did you look at it?"

"If you mean the time when the department sees visitors, from 9 a.m. to 5 p.m., there is also no footage there."

"Do your visitors not move when they are here?"

"They most certainly do," Miss Šuvaković retorted angrily. "What do you think they are, statues? And the two of us also don't sit still for eight hours. Nonetheless, it would be an unforgivable insult if we were to record our guests while they are working in our department. Do you have any idea who has access to this place? This isn't some village library where anyone can just walk in off the street. Only the most select individuals come here: academics, university professors, respected researchers. And even they have to get special permission. How could we suspect them of doing something inappropriate?"

I was tempted for a moment to respond to this, but I refrained. The conversation would be needlessly prolonged if we were to get into a discussion about the rectitude of the most select individuals, especially when confronted with the temptation of such treasures.

"I didn't have anything inappropriate in mind. In any case, there has been no theft here or any other violation of the law. I only asked whether any of your dignitaries could have perhaps left these two items here last night. Had there been any recording, we could easily have established that."

"No one left anything. I carefully inspect the entire department after the visitors leave. This was not here last night."

Silence took over the room. The two women looked at me fixedly, expecting me to say something, since we had apparently exhausted all possible explanations for the mysterious appearance of the enigmatic objects in the most secure room of the National Library. I would have said something, but I was impeded by my recent experience. I had already acted rashly once that morning by relying on Occam.

Occam offered a simple solution here too. It was easiest for Miss Šuvaković to carry all this out. She had been first to come in this morning, bringing the book and envelope with her. At that point the nighttime video surveillance was already switched off in the department. She had placed the two items on the desk, covered them with the white cloth, and assumed the role of the bewildered deputy.

However, I could not accuse her of this because I didn't have any evidence, nor did I have any clue as to what her motivation might be. Furthermore, if I were to leave the envelope aside for the moment—the issue of the book remained. Where did she get it? Why would she bring it here at all? If moving around volumes at the City Cemeteries Administration archive was only an opportune game when compared to the envelope, at the National Library this could not be the case. Who would leave behind an extremely expensive incunabulum for the sake of playing games?

All I could do was resort to the same tactics as at the City Cemeteries Administration—buy time.

"We have to carry out an investigation into how this appeared." I pointed towards the book and the envelope. "That could take a while. . . ."

"You don't understand. . . ." said Miss Šuvaković in a raised voice, interrupting me. Nonetheless, she didn't have the opportunity to continue because she was in turn interrupted by Mrs. Ognjanović, who lifted her hand again.

"Allow me, Olivera. I will explain it to the inspector. The investigation cannot take a while. We have very strict procedures in place. Not only is it prohibited to take the books from our collection out of here, there is also a careful procedure for bringing in new ones. Among other things, the origin of each edition must be precisely known. This is the basis of the Department's reputation. It would be destroyed if word were to get around that we have an exceptionally rare incunabulum with an enigmatic origin, which apparently materialized on this desk."

"Word doesn't need to get around. Only the three of us know about it, right? I will personally carry out the investigation as discreetly as possible. In the meantime, you should move the book somewhere. Perhaps it is best that you remove it from the department, since its presence here. . . ."

"Are you insane?!" shouted the deputy, again not allowing me to finish my sentence. "You don't know what you are saying! To remove an incunabulum. . . ."

"Olivera, Olivera, calm down. The inspector didn't have any bad intention. We won't remove it, of course. We'll hide it somewhere here. But this can only be temporary, a day or two at the most. I beg you to clarify everything that has happened as quickly as possible, Inspector. As quickly as possible."

"I'll do my best."

"Well, and what about this other one?" She jerked her chin in the direction of the envelope. "Is that a book inside there too?"

I shrugged. "How could I know?"

"It's addressed to you."

"You don't think that I expected a package delivered here, do you?"

She scowled at me. "It looks like a book. Would you like to check?"

"I'd rather not. Not everything that looks like a book is a book. My colleagues from the anti-terrorist department should check it first."

The two women simultaneously stepped back from the desk.

"Take that out of here," Miss Šuvaković squealed instantly.

I nodded. "Right away."

I took out a pair of plastic gloves and put them on, then lifted the envelope extremely carefully. Carrying it with my arms held out, I moved towards the elevator. I had to wait in front of the doors for the deputy to muster the courage to come and open them. She stepped aside to let me through. Standing as far back from the elevator as she could, she pressed the box with the zero, then retreated hastily.

~ 9 ~

As soon as the elevator doors closed, I lowered my hands and put the envelope under my arm. Even though I didn't feel like laughing, I couldn't hold back a smile. Miss Šuvaković's terrified face was irresistibly comical. I was still smiling when I passed through the lobby. I glanced left and nodded to the receptionist, who looked on in confusion.

When I got into my car, I placed the envelope on the passenger seat and took off the gloves. On my way out of the parking lot, the guard waved to me as though we were old friends. In front of the ramp three cars waited for a space. Through slightly lighter traffic than on the way over, I headed back to the Police Headquarters.

What had started out as a simple case had now become complicated. True, Mr. Trpimirović was not exactly the usual weirdo, the likes of which occasionally beleaguered me. If nothing else, he would have had to make a considerable investment in order to procure the strange white book. However, I had no clue as to why he had done it, what his ulterior motive was. If the purpose was to get me involved, he had only partially succeeded. To be precise, nothing was stopping me from simply removing myself from the entire affair. Since there was no violation of the law, what had occurred at the City Cemeteries Administration was no longer any of my concern. There were no grounds for an investigation.

The appearance of the second envelope, most likely with a new white volume, at the National Library Department of Old and Rare Books primarily meant that Mr. Trpimirović was not alone in all of this. He certainly was not among the dignitaries who had access. He had to have an accomplice, and that could only be the deputy administrator. No one else had had the opportunity to bring in the envelope unnoticed.

Deep underground, however, it was not only the envelope that was left, but also the incunabulum, of whose existence nobody knew. Plotting with Miss Šuvaković, Mr. Trpimirović could have procured two white books—but not such an exceptional volume. Even if they could have acquired it in some miraculous way, would they simply squander it like this? Being a weirdo has its limits too. Whatever they may have contrived, the gains they expected had to be negligible compared to such a treasure.

A sudden thought made me raise my foot off the gas pedal. The sound of hard breaking and angry honking came from behind me.

Was the thick dark-red small-format volume actually what I had been led to believe? The inscription had faded from the cover, and I wasn't permitted to open the incunabulum and see for myself the title that was printed inside. I had taken for granted what Mrs. Ognjanović had told me—that it was *The Book of Resurrection*.

However, if this wasn't true—if it was an ordinary old book—then a number of difficult questions would simply disappear. Where did the second copy of the incunabulum come from? Why would someone give up ownership of it? Finally, why specifically that book?

On the other hand, the circumstances were growing more intricate because Miss Šuvaković could not have pulled off the underground performance on her own. The administrator had to take part in it, and that already meant a genuine conspiracy. At least three people had conspired to involve me in an intrigue the sense of which completely eluded me.

Fortunately, there was a simple way to eliminate at least one perplexity. I would return to the Department of Old and Rare Books and demand to see for myself whether it truly was a 15th century edition of *The Book of Resurrection*. If it turned out not to be, I would threaten them all. Actually, the best thing would be for me to appear down there again holding the envelope at arm's length. . . .

I had already started to look for the best place to turn the car around and go in the opposite direction when my work phone rang.

I took out the telephone and looked at the screen: Mr. Grubijanić, head of the lab.

"Hello?"

"Inspector Lukić, can you stop by the lab again? It's urgent."

I wanted to ask at least two questions, but I just answered: "I'll be there in a few minutes."

∽ 10 ∾

IN ADDITION TO MR. Grubijanić, a stocky balding man in his early fifties, I also found Vesna Uskoković, the new chief inspector, in the lab. They were sitting at the table across from the entrance.

Someone who didn't know her would never think that this fragile woman, with straight blond hair and small light eyes, nearing the age of fifty, even worked for the police, let alone that she held such a high position. She looked more like a humble solfeggio teacher.

Her soft, quiet voice contributed to such an impression. Nevertheless, unlike most police officers she didn't need a strong voice in order to act authoritatively.

She had been appointed head of the city police eight months earlier, after Chief Inspector Đorđević took early retirement, immediately after the conclusion of the "Grand Manuscript" case. Even though he was not criticized officially for anything related to the case, it appeared that he was in fact advised to step down, to which he gladly acceded, all the more so because he would reach mandatory retirement in a few years' time.

His office trademark, the large aquarium, had disappeared along with him, and the new chief inspector had brought her own—a large cage with two white parrots. I'd expected her to call me in for a lengthy one-on-one talk, but she was satisfied with a short conversation that we had during the meeting where all the inspectors were introduced to her. At the time she didn't mention the two cases that set me apart from my other colleagues. She had probably learned elsewhere everything that she wanted to know.

The "Grand Manuscript" case had been concluded in the same manner as the "Last Book." My report, in which I faithfully recounted everything, was simply acknowledged. No clarification or supplement was requested. I had once more to vow that I would keep in the strictest confidence everything that I knew. I went back to my regular duties as inspector.

No one even interviewed Vera, even though I had not kept her role a secret. In any case, how could I?

"Hello, Inspector Lukić," the chief inspector said quietly. "Please, have a seat."

She indicated the chair on my right, in front of one of two large monitors. The other was between the two of them. I sat down and placed the envelope on the table. For a moment I thought about whether to remove the plastic gloves, which I had put back on after parking the car in the garage minutes earlier, but I left them on. My eyes lingered on the monitor which displayed a mosaic of images. I didn't realize right away that they were from cameras installed throughout the Police Headquarters building.

"You met with Ana Mirković twice today," the chief inspector said, getting right to the point. "Here and in your office. Did she seem upset or unusual in any way?"

I reflected for a moment, then shook my head. "No, she didn't."

"Did she perhaps say something about herself?"

"What do you mean?"

"Anything at all."

"With the exception of work, we only spoke briefly about literature. If that counts. . . ."

"About literature?" she repeated inquisitively.

"About Saramago. Perhaps you've heard of him. The Portuguese Nobel laureate who. . . ."

"I've read everything by Saramago. Did our colleague perhaps mention that she had to go somewhere? Outside of Headquarters building?"

"No, on the contrary. She said that she would be here, in the lab. Why are you asking me all this?"

The chief inspector looked at the head of the laboratory.

"Because we don't seem to be able to find Ms. Mirković. She's disappeared."

I shook my head. "How could she disappear?"

"That's precisely what we are trying to determine."

Mr. Grubijanić cleared his throat.

"I called her about fifteen minutes after you left. She would always let me know when she would leave the lab for any longer period of time. However, her phone was out of service."

"I don't understand. You don't switch off your work cell phone during office hours."

"It wasn't just turned off. I asked our colleagues from

the Communications Department for assistance. If she had only switched off her telephone, they would have gotten through to her. They told me that the cell phone is dead; as though its battery has been removed."

"Why would she remove the battery?"

"Perhaps she didn't," the chief inspector interjected. "Cell phones also appear dead when they sustain serious damage."

"You think. . . ." I started, then stopped, ". . . .that something has happened to her?"

"We don't know. However, if it has—it happened here, at Headquarters."

"How do you know?"

"We've checked footage from all the exits. She didn't leave the building. So, she's still in here, and we have no idea where."

I slapped the side of the monitor in front of me.

"You can check the recordings from the other cameras too. The entire building is covered. You'll surely get a lead on her."

"We've already checked, Inspector Lukić. This is what we've learned."

She leaned towards the monitor and her fingers danced across the keyboard. Instead of a mosaic, the monitor in front of me displayed the image of an empty corridor. It again took me a little time to recognize the view—the fifth floor. The upper right-hand corner displayed the time—10:41:26.

The image was frozen briefly, but then came to life when Ana Mirković emerged from my office. She went to the right-hand one of the two elevators and pressed the call button. The doors opened immediately and she stepped inside. As soon as they closed, the shot changed.

This time I immediately realized what I was looking at, because I had just passed by that place. The camera covered the entrances to the two elevators in the garage. Everything was still except the clock in the corner. Less than half a minute later the doors to the right-hand elevator opened, where the girl was supposed to be—but the car was empty.

I raised my puzzled gaze from the monitor. "How is this possible? Judging by the time stamp, the elevator arrived directly from the fifth floor."

"That's right. If the elevator doesn't make any stops, the descent to the basement lasts twenty-six seconds," the chief inspector said.

I stared at her bleakly. "So where is the girl?"

"We too would like to know that."

"There are no cameras in the elevators, right?"

"No, unfortunately."

"What now? What will you do?"

"We will conduct an investigation. I will personally head it. We have to find Miss Mirković as soon as possible. She can't simply disappear from the elevator at the Police Headquarters." She stopped for a moment. "Just one more question, Inspector Lukić. What was Ana doing for you this morning?"

"She was checking a book for fingerprints." I looked across the table, then nodded towards the white volume, which was still where I had left it, next to the device with two eyepieces. "That one."

"The book has already been to the lab. We saw that on the recordings. Why did you bring it again?"

"Miss Mirković did not find any fingerprints, but she wanted to run some other tests. She didn't tell me which ones. I'd like to take it with me, if you don't have any objections."

"Do you perhaps want someone else to take a look at it?" the head of the lab asked me.

"There's no need," I said as I rose and picked up the envelope. "I was only interested in the fingerprints. I'll wait for Miss Mirković to return, then I'll bring her the book again."

I took the large volume and headed towards the

door, but the chief inspector's voice stopped me. "Does that one also need to be checked for fingerprints?" she asked, pointing towards the envelope in my hand. "I see that you're wearing gloves."

"Perhaps later," I responded. "I'd first like to take a look at it."

∽ 11 ∾

I CALLED THE ELEVATOR in the garage. One of the two cars was already there and the doors opened immediately. Deep in thought, it wasn't until I had already set a foot inside that I realized that it was the right-hand elevator. I hastily pulled back my foot, and flipped the switch on the left wall of the car. The elevator was now blocked with the doors open. Without entering, I looked around the inside.

Everything seemed normal. On the opposite side was a small mirror with my reflection in it. For months following the misfortune in the elevator at 12 Oak Street I had kept my back to this mirror, as I did to mirrors in other elevators. Even though there was nothing mysterious any more about the "Grand Manuscript" case, I couldn't shake a certain uneasiness. In order to lessen it, I would keep my eyes on the floor, especially if I was alone in the elevator.

The anxiety, which had in the meantime finally receded, now had a sudden resurgence. What had happened to Ms. Mirković during the twenty-six second ride down from the fifth floor? Generally, there were only two ways to escape from a moving elevator: up and down. I remembered the hatch in the elevator floor that the disciples of the Grand Manuscript had used. Here, however, there was no carpeting that would conceal it. The floor was covered in solidly attached tiles. I looked upward. The ceiling and the lighting fixtures also looked firm.

Even if there was a secret hatch, how could a girl who had only recently started working for the police know about it? And why would she leave the elevator that way in the first place? The investigation that the new chief inspector would be heading would have to deal with a series of difficult questions.

It was odd that Chief Inspector Uskoković had not ordered the right-hand elevator to be shut down. Perhaps she wanted to avoid creating a panic at the Police Headquarters, and believed that there was no threat here because undoubtedly many people had ridden the elevator after the girl had gone missing—and nothing had happened to them. Was it prudent to take the left-hand elevator, just in case? I had to make up my mind quickly because I had been holding the elevator for quite a while. When I once again stepped into the right car, it was with the conviction that the impending uncertainty was a lesser evil than my elevator phobia kicking in again.

As the ascent started, I hastily placed the envelope and book under my arm, then crouched and started touching with one hand the edges of the floor, along the walls. Having bare hands would have improved my sense of touch, but there was no time to remove the gloves. Next I stood up, raised my free hand and passed my fingers along the edges of the low ceiling. As expected—I didn't find anything. If there was a hatch, it was concealed perfectly.

There was no need to carry out this inspection since the colleagues sent by the chief inspector had indubitably done a thorough job. Had they discovered anything, she would have told me. However, my efforts were not in vain. I was preoccupied with something and the anxiety of the ride on an elevator where one could disappear without a trace did not have the opportunity to take hold. The car came to a stop just as I lowered my hand. Twenty-six seconds had truly passed quickly.

I nodded to my colleague who was waiting for the elevator on the fifth floor, then proceeded to my office. I put the book down on the desk and opened the new envelope. Once again it was difficult to remove the thick volume. When it was finally in my hands, I briefly inspected its exterior, quickly flipped through it, then placed it next to the first one. The two white books were absolutely identical.

It crossed my mind that this could be a problem. If for any reason I needed to know which one I had received first, I wouldn't be able to identify it. The same applied to the envelopes. It was necessary to label them somehow. I glanced across my desk and concluded that sticky notes were best suited for the task. I wrote the number one on two on them and the number two on two of them, and then stuck them on the two books and the two envelopes.

Then I wondered where to put them. They could stay on the desk, since the door was locked when I was out, but there would be issues while I was in the office. Visitors would be curious, and I didn't feel like explaining how I had come by them. My first thought was to put them in one of the four drawers, but I finally concluded that it would be best to place them in the safe; it was sitting there empty anyway.

I had just locked the safe and returned the bundle of keys to my pocket, when my private cell phone rang. I removed the plastic gloves and answered.

"Do I have the honor of speaking to an actual rich person?" I asked Vera.

"Genuine and tangible."

"Tangible? What do you mean?"

"I mean that the wealth can be touched—not the rich person, if that's what you were thinking. I was given the money in a leather briefcase. All new bills. Like in the movies."

"In the movies such payments are usually illegal."

"You will not have the satisfaction of arresting me, dear inspector. The lawyers assured me that everything is perfectly legal."

"You're still at the law office?"

"I was just getting ready to leave."

"With all that money? Should I come pick you up?"

"You amaze me, inspector. Offering a rich person private protection while on the clock. Are you aware how illegal that is? No, thank you. I'd rather take a taxi. Perhaps it's not as good as police protection, but at least it is completely legal."

I coughed.

"All right, so. . . .?"

"So?"

"What is it that you can finally do, now that you're rich? What is it that you've always dreamed of?"

"You don't cease to disappoint me, inspector. What about your insightfulness? You really can't figure it out?"

"I didn't know I was suppose to figure it out."

"Of course you are. Who else if not you? Is there anyone else who knows me better?"

I thought for a bit, then said penitently: "It's no use. I can't figure it out. I give up."

"Ah, no. You don't get to surrender. I'll offer you one more opportunity to guess it. Until seven o'clock tonight. If you don't succeed by then, I'll tell you, but I'll be really disappointed."

"Why until seven?"

"Because that is when the reception we have been invited to starts. What's more, I've promised that we would go."

"What reception?"

"A gala. They'll send a limo for us at six thirty. Nothing less befits a rich person. You will tag along with me."

"Who is holding this gala reception?"

"The buyer of the inventory and books from the Papyrus. We will finally find out who it is."

I wanted to ask something more, but my work phone rang.

"I hear it," said Vera. "And my taxi is also here. I'll call you later."

I quickly hung up one telephone and answered the other.

∽ 12 ∾

"INSPECTOR LUKIĆ," SAID MY colleague Bumbaković, "there is someone on the line asking for you—a Mr. Gvozden Vidojević. He says that he has something for you."

"Transfer the connection to my office."

I went to the desk and picked up the landline telephone, which rang immediately.

"Inspector Dejan Lukić. How can I help you?"

"Hello, Inspector Lukić," a deep male voice responded. "This is Gvozden Vidojević. It would be a good idea for us to meet." He paused for a moment. "Something . . . appeared . . . at my place. Something that belongs to you."

"What is it?" I asked, even though I could have guessed the answer.

"I don't know that. The object is in an envelope, with the inscription that it is for you. Judging by its shape, I would say that it is a book. Should I open it and take a look?"

"No. Don't touch anything. I'll come pick it up immediately. Where are you?"

"At home, 14 Oak Street, second floor, apartment 3. It's the small street in. . . ."

"I know where it is," I said, interrupting him. "I will see you soon. Thank you for calling."

"You're welcome, Inspector. I'll be waiting for you."

After putting down the receiver, I briefly looked around the office then left, locking up behind me. Once again I didn't have to wait for the elevator, and it was again the right-hand car that was there. Obviously someone had just taken it to the fifth floor. As soon as the elevator started moving, I was tempted to run my bare palms across the three walls, but I didn't because it didn't make any sense. I wouldn't have found anything. There simply could be no way out in those three directions. Twenty-six seconds passed more slowly than they had fifteen minutes earlier.

I sped out of the garage and headed towards the part of town that I had had no reason to visit in eight months. Any other day it would have been only a curious coincidence—work taking me almost to the same place where the "Grand Manuscript" case had played out. However, that was not so today. Not after everything that had transpired since this morning.

By clinging to Occam, I had underestimated events. The warning light should have gone off as soon as the white book appeared, but even after it was in my hands I had carried on with the assumption that what had happened at the City Cemeteries Administration Building was actually the act of one of the many twisted people who had been pestering me since the case of the "Last Book."

I then tried to squeeze the episode from the National Library into the same mold, even though that was an even greater stretch. Indeed, how could it have even occurred to me that two or more connected weirdoes were behind everything? Such people don't get together; they always act on their own, convinced that the entire world is against them. If there was any connection between Mr. Trpimirović, Miss Šuvaković and perhaps Mrs. Leleković and Mrs. Ognjanović, then it must be of another kind. They certainly were not the common variety paranoids or conspiracy theorists; on the contrary, they were participants in a well-devised deception. What they had carried out so far—and what they continued to carry out—was possible only with the logistical support of a serious organization. This especially applied to the performance at the Department of Old and Rare Books, if it were to turn out that the incunabulum was in fact authentic.

A fresh inspiration impelled me to raise my foot abruptly from the gas pedal for the second time today. Luckily traffic was not as dense as it had been earlier, and this time there was no sound of squealing brakes behind me. I knew only one organization capable of putting together something this complex. They had convincingly demonstrated what they were capable of in both special cases: in the "Last Book" and the "Grand Manuscript."

Perhaps the best proof of the exceptionality of the secret society was that it had emerged from both affairs without suffering any consequences, at least as far as I was aware. After the second case I had been more relentless in determining whether they had gotten their just punishment. Above all I owed that much to my colleague, Inspector Vesić. However, despite all my efforts, I did not succeed in digging up any details. I was only vaguely told that everything had been handled and that I should not pursue my inquiries.

If it was in fact the secret society that was pulling the strings of everything that had happened since this morning, then my third encounter with them was unlike the previous two. First of all, they were no longer trying to get their hands on a book or manuscript that they believed was in my possession; on the contrary, they were now leaving identical copies of a strange empty volume at different locations.

Since we still hadn't started to show our hands, and everyone I had met so far had been wrapped up in their own roles, I could not even presume why they were doing everything and why they were once again all over me. The Grand Master had still not appeared to enlighten me as to what they were plotting this time.

In any case, their two past appearances on the scene had coincided with the crossing of our reality and the author's reality. However, now there was no such crossing. And there wouldn't be any, if one were to trust the author. He had firmly promised Vera that he would not meddle any more in our world, because the price was too high; a trail of bodies remained in the wake of his meddling, even when it was well-intentioned. It would have been different if he wrote a different genre, but in detective novels someone always has to die.

I could only hope that the secret society's new plan would not lead to more deaths. Whatever they had devised, for the time being it seemed rather harmless. There were no wrongdoings, other than the fact that they didn't hesitate once more to string along a police inspector. Fortunately, the inspector had finally figured out who was responsible, and he would be able to react appropriately. In any case, they were aware of who had had the last laugh so far in our confrontations. . . .

Since there were no vacant parking spaces in front of number 14, I left my car in the familiar parking lot of number 12. As I stepped out of the car, I looked up at the row of four windows on the upper left-hand corner of the building. The two center windows were tilted open. I wondered who had moved into that small apartment after the conclusion of the "Grand Manuscript" case—the apartment that held strange memories for me.

The adjacent building had four stories and showed the ravages of time. A thick vine partially concealed the decrepit state of the façade. There was no intercom at the entrance. I opened the squeaky door and entered the dim corridor. A acid smell tickled my nostrils. Even if there had been an elevator, I still would have taken the stairs to the second floor.

Apartment number 3 was the closest to the stairwell. I rang the bell. The sharp ring sounded somehow old-fashioned.

An eyeball briefly filled the large eyehole, then a deep male voice asked "Inspector Lukić?"

"Hello again, Mr. Vidojević."

The door was opened by a short older man in a frayed dark red robe, wearing a slightly lighter bow tie and worn-out slippers. He had a small mustache and a large mole on his left cheek. Even though quite gray, his longish hair was still relatively thick.

He gave a brief nod, then stepped aside. I thought that he was letting me in, but an elderly lady in a wheelchair appeared one step behind him. A red plaid blanket covered her legs. She had a wide face, vivid blue eyes and short wavy wheat-blond hair.

"My wife, Sofija," he said, introducing her.

"Pleased to meet you, Mrs. Vidojević," I said with a bow.

She responded with a smile, without saying a word.

"This way, Inspector."

He pointed left, towards a staircase, then stepped out. As he closed the door behind him, I glanced into the apartment entrance for an instant, past Mrs. Vidojević. The walls were covered by shelves full of books.

∽ 13 ∾

HOLDING ON TO THE handrail, he walked ahead of me, down the stairs.

"Don't think poorly of Sofija for wanting to meet you. She has never seen a police inspector in person before."

"I hope she wasn't disappointed."

"Oh, no, on the contrary, she was thrilled."

I thought of asking him how he knew this when his wife had not said a word, but I restrained my detective's curiosity. Perhaps couples who live together long enough eventually became telepathic. Vera and I have been together a relatively short time, and we already sometimes understood each other without words.

We reached the ground floor. I didn't know where we were headed; the last thing I expected was that we would continue our descent. Mr. Vidojević held on to the handrail once again as we started going down into the basement.

"People are usually surprised when I introduce myself. This is not how they imagine police inspectors."

"If it's any consolation, it's the same with poets. Almost everyone gives me a suspicious look when I tell them what I do. God only knows how they picture poets."

"You are a poet?"

"There—you see. It seems unbelievable even to you."

"No, no," I rushed to clear up the misunderstanding. "I don't find it at all unbelievable. I am only pleasantly surprised. I actually have a degree in literature."

In the meantime we had reached the lower level and stopped in front of a scratched olive-green metal door. Mr. Vidojević turned his head toward me and gave me a suspicious stare.

"And you work for the police?"

I sighed. "If you only knew how many times I've been asked that question. I work where there is work available. There aren't many literary jobs, unfortunately."

"Ah, yes. The literary life certainly isn't idyllic, as many people naively believe."

He took a ring with two keys out of his robe pocket and placed the larger one in the lock. He had to pull the doorknob with his other hand to unlock it, and then lean into the heavy door in order to open it. A strong sour odor struck us from the darkness. He felt around for the switch and turned on the lights.

Extending before us was a short corridor with cellars on both sides. The front and dividing walls were made out of vertical laths. I was under the impression that we were not completely underground, but I couldn't see any windows as we walked down the corridor. We stopped in front of a relatively small cellar, next to last on the left-hand side.

"I don't know whether during your literary studies there was any mention of the downsides of the poetic profession," said Mr. Vidojević, "but you will see one now."

He used the smaller key to unlock the miniature padlock. As he pulled on the door, the bottoms of the laths scraped the cement floor, making a squeaking noise.

What I had already made out through the grated entrance was now clearly visible. Resting against the only brick wall, opposite the door, was a shelf nearly full of identical copies of a thin book with a brown hard cover. I couldn't easily guess the number, but there were certainly several hundred of them.

Mr. Vidojević was the first to enter the cellar, then invited me to join him. "Welcome to the scene of my poetic penance."

I stepped in after him, keeping my sight fixed on the brown wall. He walked up to the shelf, pulled out a copy and handed it to me. Beneath his name, written in ornate script, was the title *Small Poems of Death*, and the lower part of the cover had a picture of a yellow flower. I leafed through the book. The eighty or so pages contained a series of short poems. When I got to the end, he held out his hand. As he returned the volume to its place, an expression of discomfort appeared on this face.

"Please, don't hold it against me. I would gladly give a book to a person with a literary education, but unfortunately that is not possible. All the copies of this collection of poems have to be in this cellar."

"All of them?"

"Yes. A total of 509 copies were printed. I bought most of them from the publisher: four hundred and forty-one. He was very pleased to have the opportunity to sell them to me. It was the first sold out book of poetry that he had ever published. He even offered to print a second edition immediately, if I would also buy it up."

"Really generous of him," I said with a smile.

"It was much more difficult to find the remaining sixty-eight copies that had gone on sale. I've been searching for them for two and a half years, and I've only managed to get forty-four of them. I've been to bookstores, second-hand bookshops, booksellers, and bought every copy that I could find. Next I took out ads, offering significantly more than the book is worth, but it was all in vain. Twenty-four copies still elude me. It is like they've vanished into thin air." He suddenly lit up. "Perhaps you have one? You are a man of books, you surely have a book collection. I'll pay whatever you ask. . . ."

I shook my head, and his face grew dim.

"Unfortunately I don't. If I did, I would gladly just give it to you. I understand literary passions. Although, this is one that is seldom encountered. If it isn't indiscreet of me, why do you want to buy up all the copies of your own book?" I paused for a moment. "Are you not satisfied with it?"

"Oh, on the contrary, I am very satisfied. Moreover, I think that it is my best collection of poetry."

"Then why are you refusing to share it with readers?"

He didn't respond immediately. I could see in his eyes that he was tormented.

"It's all very strange," he finally said, with a bit more vigor. "Sofija is my first reader. She read every poem back while I was writing them, and then the collection in manuscript. She appeared fascinated. But when

I brought her the first copy of the book, her reaction was quite the opposite. She was horrified. She fell into a stupor. She stopped speaking. I didn't understand anything. It took me a long time even to get her to write something at least. She didn't give me any explanation. She only commanded me to buy up all the copies and put them in the cellar. Only when the last one is in here will she speak again. And, as I said, for two and a half years I have been searching for copies of my own book, to restore Sofija's voice. . . ."

We fell silent. It was apparent that Mr. Vidojević expected me to say something in response to this, but nothing appropriate came to mind. In the end I simply repeated his words. "It truly is very strange." I was just about to move on to the reason why I had come, when something struck me. "When you were searching for your book, did you by any chance stop by the Papyrus?"

A smile came over Mr. Vidojević's face. "Ah, the Papyrus. A dear, dear bookstore. I found there about a dozen copies of *Small Poems of Death*. I liked going to Papyrus even without that reason." He sighed. "Very few such bookstores exist, ones that have a soul. It is a pity that it shut down. Did you frequent the Papyrus?"

"Often," I replied with a nod. "I hope that you will acquire the remaining copies of your collection. If I come across one, I'll be sure to let you know immediately."

The old poet smiled again. "Thank you."

"Very well, let's see that envelope that is addressed to me. It's in here, I presume."

"Yes, yes. Behind you."

He pointed downward, next to me. I turned around and spotted the envelope standing against the inside of the front wall, right next to the door. I hadn't noticed it on my way in because I was completely captivated by the books.

"You found it here?"

"That's right. I didn't touch it. I just bent over to read what was written on it."

I looked around the small cellar. There was nothing in it except the shelf. Mr. Vidojević kept it clean.

"Did you have any reason to come down here?"

"Yes. Less than an hour ago I came down to fetch the newspaper and found a copy of *Small Poems of Death* in the mailbox. The book is thin, so it can fit through the slit. However, it wasn't wrapped, which meant that the mailman didn't bring it. Someone had acquired it somewhere for me. It's no secret that I'm searching for them. The person left it in the mailbox because they obviously didn't want me to reward them. There are still good people."

"You can find them here and there," I agreed.

"In all my excitement I rushed straight to the cellar to add the new copy to the rest. I only noticed the envelope on my way out."

I squatted by the open door and gauged the gap between the laths and then the thickness of the envelope.

"There is also no scarcity of bad people," I said as I got up. "Someone had to gain unauthorized entry to your cellar in order to leave this. The envelope could not have passed between the laths."

"No one else has a key."

I removed the key from the miniature padlock and examined it, then the other one, to the metal door.

"They wouldn't need one. This padlock can be opened with a paperclip. The same goes for the lock over there," I pointed down the corridor.

"You don't say! Well, that's dreadful. Someone could break in here and take my books. . . ."

"I don't think there's any danger of that. I keep some books in the basement too. We recently had a break-in; something was taken from every cellar. Mine was the only one that they didn't even open. I can only imagine how scornfully the burglars went around it, having seen what was inside."

"That's a very sad consolation. Still, someone came in here, as you say, even if it was with the opposite motives. Should I still change the lock and padlock? I'm sure there must be something more reliable."

"Of course, but that wouldn't be enough. In order to have any protection from break-ins, you would have to build real walls, instead of these laths. The only solution would be to move the books to the apartment, but unfortunately that is impossible, as far as I understand."

The old poet sighed. "Alas, it is." He paused for a moment. "May I ask you a question, Inspector? Why did someone choose specifically my cellar to leave this for you?"

I shrugged my shoulders. "I hope that the investigation will give us that answer."

I reached for my gloves, but didn't take them out. There was no need for them. Whoever was behind this was too clever to leave any identifying clues behind. I picked up the envelope with my bare hands.

∽ 14 ∾

I HAD JUST GOTTEN into my car in the parking lot in front of number 12 when Vera called me again.

"I just wanted to let you know that I made it home safely. No one followed or attacked us, and the taxi driver had no clue who and what he was driving. I probably seemed to him like a serious businesswoman returning from a meeting, with a briefcase full of important papers." She giggled. "Actually, that would be quite the right impression."

"I thought you would put the money in the bank first. Why do you need it at home?"

"To impress an indigent police inspector. Otherwise he would never have the opportunity of seeing so much money in one place."

"The indigent police inspector has seen much more than that, on the job."

"Perhaps, but not legally gained."

"If that makes any difference."

"It is horrible hearing something like that come out of the mouth of an officer of the law."

"People change: officers of the law, as well as book-store keepers. By the way, I just spoke to one of your acquaintances from back in the day, when you were still involved in that honorable business."

"Did you? Who was it?"

"Mr. Gvozden Vidojević."

Vera paused for a moment.

"The poet?"

"Yes."

"Dear Mr. Vidojević. He was a regular customer."

"And patient."

"Patient? Why do you say that?"

"He told me that he bought copies of his own book at the Papyrus."

"So what? The man obviously liked what he had written. There's nothing unusual about a little narcissism. Everyone loves themselves, more or less."

"But you considered others, who also bought the same book time and again, to be patients?"

"In their cases we didn't know their motivations. It could have been something weird."

"In Mr. Vidojević's case it wasn't mere narcissism either."

"What was it?"

"It's a long story. And a sad one. I'll tell you when I get back."

"Where did you speak?"

"At his place, in the basement." I sighed. "Overall, I'm spending most of my day below ground."

"Is something unusual happening?" Vera asked after a brief silence.

"Nothing especially," I responded, with the slightest hesitation. "It seems that today I'm meeting all your patients. As you know, first someone rearranged the records of the burials at the City Cemeteries Administration. Then someone else brought a rare book into the National Library. And now this thing with Mr. Vidojević. I hope that's the end of it. In any case, I don't remember any of your former patients' other peculiarities."

"Oh, there were plenty of them."

"These three are quite enough. If there is another such case, I'll start to believe that the former honest bookstore keeper—and now the bored rich person who has nothing better to do—has cast a spell on me. When will you start doing what you've always dreamed about?"

"Ah, you're curious as to what that is. Just you keep trying to figure it out, Mr. uninsightful police Inspector. You have a little over six hours left. . . ."

I returned the telephone to my jacket pocket, drove out of the parking lot and headed back to the office.

Having turned right onto Oak Street, I continued slowly to the cast iron fence beyond which two arched windows extended from the basement. I stopped the car next to the curb. Everything looked the same as it had eight months earlier, except there was no metal sign in the shape of a teapot hanging above the door. There was no reason to get out. There was no teashop there any more, and even if there had been—my memories of it were not pleasant. I drove on.

Mr. Vidojević and his wife seemed, very convincingly, to be the persons that they claimed to be. However, the same had applied to the other members of the secret society, both the ones I had previously met and those whom I had today suspected to be part of it. Furthermore, Mr. Vidojević was one of the Papyrus regular patrons, and many of them were followers of the Grand Master.

On the other hand, if this today was truly a performance put on by the secret society, its main problem was the complexity of the three acts. It was true that the society was logistically capable of carrying them out, but why would it invest so much effort and money just to deliver three books to me? I could have received them in a far simpler and cheaper way: by regular mail, for example. Unless, of course, the purpose of the performance wasn't to deliver the books but something completely different, something that was yet to be revealed. And if it was so, then new scenarios could be expected. In any case, the performance was still far from over.

I walked towards the elevator in the garage, carrying the third envelope with me. I was just about to press the call button when I wondered which door would open this time. If it was the right-hand one, and it also turned out that the elevator was already there, it would be quite incredible. When I completed the motion, however, something equally incredible happened: both doors opened.

I stood there indecisively, feeling as though I was being tested somehow. It was like I was supposed to decide something far more important and far-reaching than which elevator I would take. Who knows how long I would have stood there had the doors not started to close at the same time. Startled out of my stupor, I jumped into the left car at the last moment.

The ride to the fifth floor felt neither too long nor too short. I smiled at the two colleagues whom I met in the corridor as I walked towards my office, while taking out my key along the way. I slid the key into the lock and turned it, as I had done countless times before, ever since I was given my own office, as a sort of compensation for the promotion that I didn't receive after the "Last Book" case.

However, the key jammed after a quarter-turn.

Brows raised, I stared at the lock in confusion, then looked up and checked the number above the door, even though I was certain that I had not gotten the office wrong. Something like that had never happened to me before, and neither had it now.

Then I realized what it was: I couldn't unlock the door because it wasn't locked in the first place. I pulled out the key, turned the knob, opened the door—and saw probably the last two people I expected to find there.

∽ 15 ∾

I COULD EASILY HAVE failed to recognize the two young members of the National Security Agency. Stanislav Mirić, the information and communications technology wizard, and the photographer, who often smiled at me, had completely changed their appearances.

He no longer had unkempt hair; it was neatly combed, even slicked back. He wore an elegant suit and tie, instead of the hooded sweatshirt and sweatpants, and there was no conspicuous earring dangling from his right ear. Her black hair was no longer shaven above her ears, a dark suit replaced the torn skin-tight jeans and colorful knit vest, and gone were the rings from her lower lip, right nostril and earlobes. Even now, however, they didn't seem like agents, but rather like yuppies ready for an important meeting.

They sat in the armchairs in front of my desk. The girl had the two envelopes and two white books in her lap. I glanced at the safe where I had left them. It was closed.

"It seems that fashions change often at the National Security Agency," I said as I made my way to the chair on the opposite side of the desk. Along the way I dropped the third, still unopened envelope into the girl's lap. There was no sense in trying to keep it, especially since they had come for it. I got a brief smile in return.

"Not only fashions, Inspector Lukić," Mirić responded. "There are also other, greater changes. For example, Commissioner Milenković is no longer with us."

"Is that so?" I asked in surprise. "Why is that?"

"He was retired after the last case that we cooperated on."

"What was he blamed for? Didn't he do everything that he could under the circumstances?"

"He wasn't blamed for anything. He retired at his own request. It seems that he was just worn out. As you are well aware, this is a very exhausting job, and his age had caught up with him."

"So, that's what happened. We've had similar cases where people retired at their own request, because of exhaustion and age. And who is your Commissioner now, if I may ask?"

"You may ask, but I cannot answer. In any case, the two of us have been assigned this new case because of our experience with the previous one. Regardless of the fact that it didn't end well."

"What new case?"

The two of them looked at each other.

"Inspector Lukić," she said to me, "we don't want to make the same mistake that Commissioner Milenković made. Based on the two previous cases, it is clear to us that we must genuinely cooperate with you in order to get anything done. I solemnly promise that we will not keep anything from you, if you are completely open with us in return. We can all only benefit from true cooperation."

"And this is a good way to start true cooperation?" I pointed to the books and envelopes in her lap. "You break into my office, and my safe, and just take everything from it. Commissioner Milenković did have an unusual understanding of cooperation, but he never did anything like this."

"We removed the books in order to safeguard them. They are not secure in your safe. Someone else could have gotten a hold of them as easily as we did, and we have to assume that they are very important. We also wanted our experts to take a look at them. Still, they will be made available to you whenever you need. Also, if we had dishonorable intentions, we would not be here waiting for you, would we?"

I looked at the girl for several moments without saying a word.

"It isn't easy for me to trust the honorable intentions of someone whose name I don't even know."

A shadow of reluctance passed over her face, as though she had been asked to disrobe in front of a stranger.

"Senka Veselinović," she said finally, blushing slightly.

"I'm glad to make your acquaintance, Agent Veselinović," I responded with a smile. "Very well, now let me repeat my question—what new case?"

"The new case of crossing realities," Mirić said. "Three extremely unusual books have mysteriously appeared. It might be possible to find an explanation for two of them, but not for the third—the one from the National Library Department of Old and Rare Books. Not to mention the incunabulum."

I was again briefly silent.

"How long have you been following me?"

"We've never let you out our sight. For eight months. Both previous cases started with you, so it was natural to assume that the third, if there ever was one, would too. As soon as you got the call from the City Cemeteries Administration about problems involving books, the alarm was raised. And we weren't wrong."

I sighed. "I think you were. This cannot be a new case of crossing realities."

"Why can't it?" the girl asked.

"The fact that the cases start with me is beside the point. The much more important issue is that there need to be dead bodies. The author who is pulling the strings from the other reality writes detective novels, and you simply can't have one without murder victims. Just remember how many there were in *The Last Book* and *The Grand Manuscript*. Nonetheless, this time no one is dead."

"Not yet," Mirić remarked, "but victims could still appear. In *The Grand Manuscript* quite some time passed before the first corpse turned up."

"Perhaps, but until that happens, we cannot dismiss other possibilities, besides crossing realities."

"What other possibilities?"

I glanced from the young man to the girl and back again.

"There is someone else capable of pulling off everything that has happened today. Even the thing at the National Library. You know, of course, who I'm talking about—the Grand Master and his secret society."

I paused, expecting them to say something, but they just gazed at me in silence.

"If we are truly to cooperate, then the time has come for you to show that you are actually prepared to do so. You have to answer one question: how is it that the secret society got away scot-free in the first two cases?"

This time agents Veselinović and Mirić looked at each other a bit longer.

The girl finally cleared her throat and turned towards me.

"Someone is protecting them. Someone very influential. We really don't know who it is. Whenever the Agency tries to take action against them, our efforts are thwarted. Without any explanation. After the "Grand Manuscript" case, Commissioner Milenković wanted to get revenge against the Grand Master, even more than against the author, because he had insolently taken both him and the service for fools, but he wasn't allowed to. That is the main reason why he took retirement."

For a brief moment it was as though no one knew what to say.

"Yet there is something," the young man spoke up, "that the secret society could not pull off, regardless of how powerful it might be."

I shook my head. "What?"

"It couldn't make your colleague Ana Mirković disappear from a moving elevator."

"Perhaps, but that event is not linked to the others."

"You think so?" the girl asked.

"All right, perhaps it is, but don't underestimate the secret society when it comes to elevators. I personally saw how skilled they are. In any case, who knows what happened in that elevator. The new chief inspector has decided to handle that personally. We'll see what her investigation uncovers. A pity there wasn't a camera inside. We would easily have solved the mystery."

A fresh pause ensued.

"There was," Mirić finally said softly.

"Excuse me?" I asked in disbelief.

"We would never have told you if we were not truly cooperating, Inspector Lukić," said Agent Veselinović. "The camera is hidden behind the mirror. I ask that this remain strictly between us."

I nodded. "Of course, of course. And what did it capture?"

The girls put her hand in her bag and pulled out a large tablet.

"Here, take a look."

I rose to take it, then sat back down. The image on the tablet was frozen. It showed Ms. Mirković, who had just gotten on the elevator on the fifth floor. The door behind her was still open. I touched the round icon with an arrow at the bottom of the screen and the image came to life.

The young lady first pressed the lowest button on the left-hand row, then went to the mirror and looked at her face curiously, obviously looking for something that she could touch up. However, there was no time for beautification because everything went dark as soon as the doors behind her came together in the center.

There was no sound. I stared at the monotonous darkness which was interrupted only by the small digits of the clock in the upper right-hand corner. It measured even thousandths of a second. At the moment when the lights went back on in the elevator, the clock stopped at 00:26:118. The car was empty.

I continued to stare at the image on the tablet, which was frozen again, then got up and handed it back to Agent Veselinović.

"What happened?" I asked as I sat down.

"We have no idea," Agent Mirić responded. "It isn't normal darkness. If it were, we would see at least something in it. The camera is infrared. It would show the girl's face radiating heat."

"Such an image" his colleague added, "would be produced if someone were to have covered the mirror with something opaque, but it wouldn't have foiled the camera's microphone. It is very sensitive, it would have picked up even the faintest sound. However, it didn't capture anything; it is as though the girl had stood there motionless, not even breathing."

"The clock in the corner," I said after thinking for a moment, "is it part of the recording or was it added later?"

Agent Veselinović looked at her colleague questioningly.

"It was added later. Why do you ask?" he responded.

"Then there is another explanation. The camera and microphone were switched off for the twenty six seconds of the elevator's descent."

"That simply isn't possible. In order to get to the

camera, one would have first to remove the mirror, and it would have captured that."

"The camera can also be reached from behind, without removing the mirror."

Agent Mirić watched me carefully for several moments, then shook his head. "While the elevator was in motion and in such a short time? Impossible."

"Not then, but beforehand. If the secret society had decided to switch off your cameras when it needed to, it would have taken care of that in time."

"In the middle of the Police Headquarters building?" the girl asked in disbelief.

"Even in the middle of the National Security Agency building. They are by no means to be underestimated. It would be best for you to check whether your hidden cameras have some upgrades that you are not aware of."

The young man sighed. "Even if it were as you say, Inspector Lukić, we still face two very difficult questions. First, how did the secret society pull off the disappearance of the girl from a moving elevator in less than half a minute? All right, perhaps they have installed something that switched off the cameras, but they could not remove someone from an elevator that doesn't have any secret hatches. We are positive about that. Second, why would it undertake something so complex only to make someone so insignificant disappear?"

"Perhaps she isn't insignificant," I responded, just to have an answer.

To my great surprise, Agent Mirić nodded. "I agree, she's important. That is to say, she will be soon. As soon as we find her dead somewhere. Perhaps even in the elevator from which she mysteriously vanished. A corpse will be the last missing piece to complete this—the new detective novel by the author from the other reality."

I opened my mouth to contradict him, but my work cell phone rang.

"Hello?"

That was all I said. Fifteen seconds later I hung up and returned the telephone to my pocket. I then looked first at one young face across from me, then at the other. I stood up without a word, and at that moment their cell phones rang.

"Let's go," I said before someone else could give them the news. "Ms. Mirković has been found."

~ 16 ~

THEY STILL ANSWERED THEIR phones. Like me, they restricted themselves to listening. They skipped even the opening "hello." After about half a minute they both hung up. They stayed seated.

"You go ahead, Inspector Lukić," said Agent Mirić. "We'll be just a moment."

I wrinkled my eyebrows. What seemed so important to them, right now, in my office, that it was more pressing than the appearance of the girl? Still, I didn't ask them because I considered the latter to be more important. Who knows whether they would even tell me, despite the new openness between us. I just shrugged and rushed out of the door.

For some reason I was convinced that at least one elevator would be there, but it took a good three minutes for the left-hand one to arrive. I pressed the lowest button and stood with my back to the mirror. It didn't stop at any of the other floors, so I reached the garage in half a minute. The right-hand car was standing there with the doors open, as though the elevator was blocked or shut down.

I briskly opened the basement door and burst into the corridor. Three of my colleagues curiously watched me run by. This is already the second time today, I thought to myself. I rushed into the lab, again without knocking.

The only person inside was the chief. He was seated on the other side of the large table, as he had been the previous two times.

"Where is she?" I asked, while looking around in confusion.

"At the infirmary. The chief inspector took her," answered Mr. Grubijanić, who was the one who had notified me that Ms. Mirković had returned.

"Is she hurt?"

"No. At least she wasn't complaining of anything. Chief Inspector Uskoković still wanted a doctor to take a look at her." He paused. "Have a seat, Inspector Lukić."

I hesitated for a moment, then pulled out the nearest chair and sat down.

"What happened?"

The head of the lab sighed.

"We have no idea. The girl just turned up about twenty minutes ago. As though she had been absent for only a short while, she went back to her workstation," he pointed towards the part of the table where the instrument with two eyepieces stood, "and pored over her work. She was shocked when I told her what time it was. She was convinced that it was quarter to eleven, not almost one thirty."

I stared at Mr. Grubijanić for several moments.

"Did she say anything about the elevator ride?"

"Only that it was quite normal. She got on at the fifth floor, pressed the button for the basement and arrived here without stopping at any other floor. Nothing special happened."

"Did you take a look at the footage of her coming out of the car? Where did the elevator come from?"

"That is another mystery—from nowhere. It was already on the basement level. Two of our colleagues had taken it down several minutes before. The elevator remained here because no one had called it from above.

Then the doors opened again—and Ms. Mirković stepped out."

"They are still open."

"Yes, the chief inspector ordered that the elevator be shut down."

"Perhaps she should have done it sooner, as soon as the girl disappeared."

"How then would she have come back?"

I was left speechless again for a moment.

"Good question," I replied with a nod.

From behind me came the sound of the door opening. I turned around quickly and found myself facing Ms. Mirković. She stopped for an instant, smiled sheepishly as though she were justifying herself for some reason, shut the door behind her and turned to the left. She looked quite normal, as she had this morning. She sat down, briefly stared in front of her, then looked first at her boss, and then at me.

"How are you?" was all that I could think of.

A smile passed over her face again. "Fine, thanks."

"What did the doctor tell you?"

"That I should spend more time in the sun. Other than that, everything is all right."

I paused a second before speaking again. Without my even intending it, my voice grew softer.

"How was it . . . in the elevator?"

She shrugged. "Like always." It seemed that was all she had to say, then she added: "I smiled once."

"Did you?" I asked curiously.

"I remembered a funny sentence from Saramago's novel about death."

Before I could ask which one, the girl turned to her superior.

"The chief inspector suggested that I go home, but I said that I'd rather stay. I hope you have nothing against that."

"As you wish."

"Can I take a look at your . . . book, Inspector Lukić?"

"There are now three of them. Unfortunately, none of them are in my possession any more."

The girl continued looking at me, expecting me to say something else, but at that moment my work cell phone rang again. I was a little clumsy taking it out. Instead of the caller ID, a number appeared on the screen.

"Hello?"

"Inspector Lukić," said a flustered female voice, "this is Hristina Leleković, Administrator of the City Cemeteries Administration. You must come immediately. Something dreadful has happened."

~ 17 ~

I DIDN'T LEARN WHAT the dreadful thing that had happened was, because she immediately hung up. I returned the telephone to my pocket and rose.

"Please excuse me, something has come up. I'd like to come back later to chat, if you don't mind."

"I don't mind, Inspector. I'll be here."

As I left the laboratory, I thought of how she had already told me that once before. I hoped that this time she would not be foiled in such an extraordinary way.

I didn't turn on the police light, as I would have done in any other emergency. Mrs. Leleković sounded agitated, but it had been the same this morning, and there turned out to have been no reason for haste. It was quite possible that she'd avoided telling me what trouble had befallen the City Cemeteries Administration because then I might not have come at all. In any case, I didn't need the police light to get through the sparse traffic.

The mysterious disappearance of Ms. Mirković from the moving elevator was only a conjuring trick compared to the fact that she had experienced the passing of almost three hours as only half a minute. The secret society might have been able to pull off the former by some form of prestidigitation, but not the latter. Or perhaps it could? I knew very little about hypnosis, so I didn't know whether someone in such a state could be convinced that actually much less time had passed.

I shook my head, as I occasionally do when I ponder a problem. I did this while standing at an intersection, waiting for the light to change. An older lady in the car to my left looked distrustfully at the weird guy talking to himself. Occam would have scolded me for accumulating increasingly complex assumptions like this. It was necessary to look for a significantly simpler one.

The moment I set off from the intersection, the simplest solution occurred to me. There was no need for hypnosis, and the disappearance from the elevator, however it may have occurred, would certainly be significantly simpler to pull off if my young colleague was a accomplice, and not a victim in the secret society's performance. Occam would have liked this. The girl's odd literary taste—funny novels about death—supported this possibility.

The only opponent of this idea was my intuition. As a rational person I had to dismiss it, since nothing supported it. I would have already done so had my intuition not proven to me on several occasions that the solution does not necessarily always have to be arrived at by following Occam.

Preoccupied with the enigma of how the performance in the elevator had been carried out, I had lost track of perhaps a more important question—why had it been set up in the first place? The secret society makes a huge effort to organize the seemingly impossible disappearance of a member of the police staff from an elevator—regardless of whether she took part in the performance or not—only to simply return her. What was the meaning of this? What did they aim to achieve?

And why were they playing hide-and-seek with me? On the previous two occasions when our paths had crossed, they immediately let me know what they wanted—*The Last Book* and *The Grand Manuscript*. Now they were nowhere to be seen, leaving me to speculate about their intentions. And they certainly had something in mind; they were not doing all this just to toy with me. It was high time that they came out of the shadows and revealed their hand.

The area around the City Cemeteries Administration Building was bustling as usual. There were considerably more cars than there were parking spaces. Even though I did so reluctantly, this time I had no choice: I stopped the car where it was explicitly forbidden, took out my police light and placed it on the roof. It would serve a purpose after all.

There was quite a few of people in the corridor, but the guard noticed me immediately. He waved to me from the glass booth, then reached for the telephone. He put down the receiver after a few words and came out.

"The administrator is on her way," he said with a squint. "She'll blame me again. . . ."

"What happened?"

He looked at me as though to ask "Don't you know?" Then his eyes turned for a moment to the stairway leading to the basement.

"The administrator will explain everything to you. I'm not authorized." He paused, then repeated: "It's not my fault."

I wanted to calm him, but at that moment, just like this morning, a piercing "Mr. Rabrenović!" reverberated from behind me. Many heads turned towards the administrator, who was approaching from the left with a crisp step. The guard swiftly retreated to the booth.

"It took you a while to get here again, Inspector."

"Perhaps I would have come faster had I known why I had been summoned this time."

"I told you that something dreadful has happened."

"It would have been more helpful if you had told me what exactly had happened. Then I would have assessed how dreadful it actually was and I would have adjusted the speed of my arrival accordingly."

"You should have relied on my assessment. Anyway, we don't have time for this sparring. Come this way."

∽ 18 ∽

SHE WALKED AHEAD OF me, towards the basement. On reaching it, I saw a man standing in front of the last door on the left.

"You may go now," the administrator told him as we approached. "I'll call you shortly."

She waited for the large older man to move away.

"I told Mr. Rosić to guard the archive until the lock-smith comes to replace the lock."

"What happened to the lock?" I couldn't see it; the administrator obscured it by standing in front of the door.

"It's broken. We had to break in."

She stepped back. At first glance everything seemed fine. Then I bent down and noticed cracks in the door-frame.

"Why did you break in?"

She glanced at the corridor behind me, as though making sure that we weren't overheard. Even though there was no one there, she continued in a softer voice.

"To see what was going on with Mr. Trpimirović. I arrived around one o'clock. I knocked, but he didn't open. I thought that he might have gone to the re-stroom. He was required to notify me if he was going anywhere else. . . ."

"Quite a strict regimen," I said, interrupting her.

"It wouldn't do the police any harm either. In any case, I returned about fifteen minutes later; again he didn't answer my knock. I sent Mr. Rosić to check whether Mr. Trpimirović was in the men's room. I thought that he might have fallen ill, even though he is in excellent health, contrary to your unseemly insinuation that the lack of daylight might be harming him."

She paused, giving me a sullen stare.

"He wasn't in the restroom?"

"No, he wasn't. Why else would we have broken in?"

"It would have been simpler for you to presume that he had in fact gone out. Even the healthiest of people ultimately break under too strict a regimen."

"You don't know Mr. Tripimirović. He would never do that. We assumed something much more likely— that he had fallen ill inside. That would not have been strange. He had a very stressful start to the day. Among other things, he was unjustly accused."

"Well, did you find him in the archive?"

She just stared at me for a moment without saying a word, then shook her head.

"There, you see—in the end he got sick and tired of your regimen."

"Don't be so quick to gloat, Inspector Lukić. There was no one in the archive, but there was something that could not have got there under any circumstances."

It was now I who stared for several moments, overcome by the premonition that I had jumped to a conclusion for the second time, in this same place.

"What?" I finally asked.

"A key in the lock."

I felt something tickle the back of my neck.

"It was locked from the inside, and there was no one in the room?"

"Precisely so. Mr. Trpimirović had disappeared from the archive, which was locked from the inside. Didn't I tell you that something dreadful had happened?"

"You should have called me before you broke in."

"We feared for Mr. Trpimirović. Every moment

could have been precious, and you aren't exactly famous for your swift arrivals."

I sighed and shook my head.

"Who all has been inside?"

"Just Mr. Rosić and myself."

"Did you touch anything?"

"Absolutely nothing."

I took out my plastic gloves and put them on.

I entered the archive and examined the lock first. The signs of the break-in were more visible on the inside; the key protruded halfway. I went over to the desk. Everything looked as it had this morning: the large open book, documents, inkwell, pen, vase. I crossed to the first bookcase. The volumes were now arranged properly.

The administrator stood outside the open door and watched me without saying a word. I looked around the room, then surveyed the bookcases. They were the only other thing to look at. I stopped in the middle of the third wall. The monotonous dark gray panorama was interrupted by a void: a volume was missing. I took out my cell phone and took a close-up picture. Mrs. Leleković leaned in a little to see what had attracted my attention. Two bookcases down I again found an empty space and took another picture.

Having completed a full circuit, I looked at the ceiling and the floor. Then I came out, closed the door behind me and removed the plastic gloves. I didn't return the telephone to my pocket, but retreated to a discreet distance from the administrator and called the crime scene team, giving them instructions in a low voice.

"My colleagues are coming to process the scene," I said upon returning to the door of the archive. "Please make sure that no one goes in, including yourself."

For a moment she seemed ready to protest, but then she nodded. "All right."

"By the way, have you noticed that there are two volumes of burial records missing—3361 and 3521?"

"You don't say?" she answered, shocked, then immediately justified herself. "I most certainly would not have overlooked that, but I was very upset by the disappearance of Mr. Trpimirović. It's so dreadful. . . ."

"It's not exactly dreadful. You have the digital archives. You can make a copy of whatever is missing. If it is necessary at all. Perhaps Mr. Trpimirović has the books."

She squinted at me briefly.

"What do you mean? Where is Mr. Trpimirović? What has happened to him?"

"He's not inside, which means that he had to leave somehow."

"But the door was locked from the inside."

"It's possible to escape even from locked rooms." For a moment I was tempted to add that I had recently encountered such a case, but I restrained myself.

"How?"

"Through a window, for example."

"The windows are covered by bookcases, and there are also bars on them."

"Then there must be another way out."

Her voice grew stern again. "That's preposterous! I should know this building if anyone does. There is no other way out of the archive."

"In that case the only thing we can do is to conclude that Mr. Trpimirović simply vanished into thin air. Does that seem more acceptable to you?"

She opened her mouth but couldn't come up with a response, so closed it again. Her eyes blazed.

"I suggest you remain patient. My people will be here soon. Let them check whether there is another way out. The building was originally a private villa, right? They often have secrets that later owners or tenants have no clue about. Stay here until they arrive, please. I will call you as soon as I get the report from the crime scene team."

Without waiting for her to say anything else, I turned and walked off down the corridor at a brisk pace, then ran up the stairs to the ground floor. I was already at the entrance when I heard a muffled shout behind me.

"Inspector!"

I turned towards the guard, who was approaching from the direction of the booth. Before reaching me he looked right and left at the people who were in the corridor just then.

"Do you have a minute?" he asked. "I'd like to show you something."

I looked him over briefly, then nodded.

"This way."

He motioned towards the stairwell. Thinking that he would go into the basement, I was about to warn him that the administrator was still there, which he certainly would not appreciate, but he headed up the stairs. On reaching the second floor, he glanced in both directions first, just as he had downstairs. There was no one around at that moment.

The floor was identical to the two lower levels in every respect—the same row of doors on both sides, the same thick red-and-yellow carpeting. We headed left and soon reached the end of the corridor. When he turned the doorknob on the last door on the left, I thought that he was taking me into an office, but a new staircase appeared beyond it. It was wooden and seemed rather old. Since this was a two-story building, this was obviously the way up to the attic.

He paused with his foot on the first step and turned towards me.

"This remains in the strictest confidence, Inspector. I would be fired immediately if they learned that I'd brought you here."

"Don't worry."

The stairs creaked under our feet as we climbed up. The low door at the top of the stairs also seemed dilapidated. The attic had obviously not been included in the renovation project for the City Cemeteries Administration.

The guard searched briefly in his right pants pocket before taking out a key. He slid it into the lock, but had difficulty turning it. He muttered something. He finally unlocked the door, and with a fresh creak pulled it towards him and slipped inside.

"Come in quickly and close it behind you," he said from the darkness. "Someone might come along downstairs. I'll turn on the light right away."

I complied. Surrounded by murky obscurity, I remained by the door. I heard Rabrenović moving about at an indeterminate distance in front of me. I was just asking myself why the switch was not in the most logical place, next to the door, when there was a flash of light. Yet it wasn't regular lighting. The powerful beam of a flashlight pierced my eyes painfully, blinding me. I instinctively raised my right hand to protect myself.

Everything was calm for several moments. Then from the other end of the blade of light a deep male voice resounded, one that I had not heard in eight months.

∽ 19 ∾

"HELLO, INSPECTOR LUKIĆ," SAID the Grand Master. "Once again we meet in the dark."

"Doesn't seem that way to me," I replied, still shielding my eyes with my hand.

"Oh, forgive me." The blade instantly slid back into the sheath of darkness. "Is this better?"

Even though I was again overcome by sightlessness, the blazing image lingered on my retinas for quite a while.

"More acceptable. I was just wondering when you would show up."

"You were expecting us?"

"Could this have transpired without you? The only thing I didn't expect was that we would be brought into contact by a not-overly-conscientious guard. Congratulations, Rabrenović. I would never have suspected you."

A "thank you" could be heard from the deeper darkness.

"The others deserve commendations too. You've always had excellent actors. Are any of them here in the attic too?"

"Who do you mean?"

"You know very well who I mean: the administrator and Mr. Trpimirović, the two ladies from the National Library, Mr. and Mrs. Vidojević. The acting ensemble probably also includes my colleague, Ms. Mirković."

"You're wrong, Inspector. Those aren't at all members of our society."

"There's no need for you to pretend. We know each other well enough. Better just openly tell me what it is that you want from me this time. Why are you organizing extremely elaborate performances just to deliver empty books to me?"

The darkness remained mute for a while.

"You didn't get them from us."

"It could only be you. No one else is capable of pulling off something like that. Especially not the act at the National Library."

"Think about our previous encounters; we never gave anything to you. On the contrary, we were always trying to get something from you."

"That was in the previous two cases. Now it's the other way around, for some reason. Let me hear what you're planning. We're just wasting time playing hide-and-seek in the dark."

There was another brief bout of silence.

"I'd like to propose something," proclaimed the

Grand Master. "If you are truly convinced that you received the books from us, simply return them to us. We will disappear instantly. We won't bother you any more. I'm aware that my word doesn't mean much to you, but I'm giving it to you anyhow."

Now it was I who didn't respond immediately.

"Even if I wanted to, I couldn't," I finally said. "I no longer have them."

"The National Security Agency took possession of them, yes, but that's not a great obstacle. They told you that the books were at your disposal whenever you wanted them."

"You're very well informed, as always."

"Poorly informed persons don't go into this line of work."

"By the way, the Agency is burning with desire to know who is protecting you. It certainly must be someone exceptionally powerful. Even I am itching with curiosity as to who it might be. Would you agree to a trade—the books for that information?"

"I would not," the deep voice from the darkness responded without any hesitation. "There are much cheaper ways for us to get a hold of those books. Let the Agency keep trying to figure out who is protecting us. In any case, even if I were to agree, how could you be sure that you'd received the correct information? It cannot be verified."

"Why do you even care about those empty white books? What is it this time?"

Another short pause ensued.

"Your condescending tone is inappropriate, Inspector Lukić. We're on opposite sides, but that doesn't mean that we shouldn't respect each other. We will do anything to finally defeat you, but we greatly respect you as an adversary who has outwitted us on two occasions. It would be honorable if you could at least appreciate our goals, since you can't appreciate our means."

"It isn't only the means that are questionable, but also the fact that the goals concern only a very small number of people. You wanted to get your hands on *The Last Book* so that the members of your secret society alone might be spared the apocalypse. In the case of *The Grand Manuscript* it was even more exclusive: eternal life awaited only one person—the one who read it first. I assume that you were saving that privilege for yourself."

"If that worries you, then I have good news. There is no more discrimination. None. The empty white books, as you mockingly call them, concern all people. Without exception. And not only the living, but also the dead. Actually, primarily the dead. Do you know how many people have lived out their lives and died since mankind appeared in this world?"

Of course, I had no idea, so I gave a safe assessment. "Many."

"Many, yes. Very many. Unimaginably many. Around a hundred billion. All of them are listed in *The Compendium of the Dead*. No one has been left out."

"Then we're not talking about the same thing. There is no one listed in the three volumes that I received, and even the title was omitted."

"All that will appear when you receive the last, fourth volume."

"Ah, so. Another one is expected."

"That's right. It has to appear soon. Without it the first three are worthless. Only with the fourth does it become *The Compendium of the Dead*."

"Even if I got hold of four million more such volumes, it still wouldn't be enough to inscribe even the most basic information for a hundred billion people—nothing but their names and dates of births and deaths. And even that in the smallest possible lettering."

"I agree. However, there are also other types of records, other than alphabetic. We live in a time of quantum marvels, don't we? Four volumes made out of very special paper are sufficient to hold a lot more than the most basic data about a hundred billion people. There is enough space for a detailed biography of each of them."

"All right, let's assume that there is. But why are you interested in *The Compendium of the Dead*? What is the use of this four-volume set with quantum-inscribed information about all the people who ever existed? You must see some benefit, otherwise you wouldn't get involved in all this."

"Your negative opinion of us is clouding your perspective, Inspector Lukić. We don't have any benefit in mind. We only want to prevent the disaster that would inevitably occur if *The Compendium of the Dead* were to fall into the wrong hands."

"What disaster?"

"This certainly is not a mere list of deceased, as it seems to you. It is a miraculous artifact that makes mankind's most ancient dream possible; the realization of the hopes that are the purpose of the existence of all great religions; the rectifying of nature's greatest mistake." He paused for a moment, for dramatic effect. "Whoever has *The Compendium of the Dead* will be able to bring back the dead."

There seemed to be some commotion in the darkness in front of me, but it was also possible that I had imagined it.

"Resurrection?" I said questioningly.

"Resurrection," the Grand Master confirmed.

I sighed. "I still don't understand what kind of disaster is looming."

"How isn't it clear to you? Imagine if *The Compendium of the Dead* fell into the hands of someone who, like you, was overly democratically oriented, and who decided to bring back to life all the deceased. This poor planet is already struggling even with seven billion people on it, and with a hundred and seven it would instantly collapse."

"So, there's no good news. You will be acting out of elitist motives once again."

"That is inevitable. There is not nearly enough space for everyone. A selection must be made. In any case, not everyone actually deserves to be resurrected. However, space would be found for the chosen. For many of the chosen. And that is actually good news, isn't it?"

"And the chosen would be selected by you, I assume?"

"It would be best that it is done by someone who is up to the job. Otherwise it could lead to disaster of another kind."

"Would the chosen also include those whom you deprived of their lives in carrying out your harebrained schemes? It would give you an opportunity to make up for the crimes you had committed in pursuit of your goals."

There was no reply from the darkness. When the deep voice was heard again it had lost its previous friendly tone.

"There would hardly be room for them on our list."

"You can go ahead and tear up your list. It's all nonsense. There is no resurrection, just as there was no end of the world or eternal life."

"How is it then that three parts of *The Compendium of the Dead* have already appeared?"

"Because you planted them. I'm sure you have a reason for doing so. Otherwise, you could have come here this morning before me and taken the first volume. You feel quite at home in this building, don't you?"

"We were a little late, unfortunately. Rabrenović did not deserve your commendation."

"And what do you have against Trpimirović? Why did you get rid of him? He did his job impeccably."

"I have nothing against him. If he were my man, I'd never get rid of him."

"You really are persistent about this."

"Just as you are in not believing me."

"We're going around in circles. Perhaps I would believe you if there were someone else who could have done everything that has occurred since this morning. But there isn't."

"You think so? It seems that your insightfulness really has faded, Inspector Lukić."

At that moment the pounding of a myriad of running feet could be heard, first from the second floor, then from the wooden stairs behind me. The commotion in the darkness before me was definite this time, but it lasted only for an instant. When the door flew open, there was only a squinting police inspector in the attic.

∽ 20 ∼

A LARGE GROUP BURST in. There was a good deal of confusion, even though no one spoke. Several flashlight beams wandered around, appropriating small patches of visibility from the darkness. One pointed briefly at my face, blinding me again. I covered my eyes with my hands for a second time, and it was just then that someone flipped the light switch behind me. I lowered my hands but my loss of sight lasted a few more seconds.

Upon recovering it, I finally saw the large attic where I had spent the past ten or so minutes in complete darkness. There were no partition walls, only a series of load-bearing columns and horizontal cement beams supporting the roof. The space was almost completely empty. In the rear and to the right was a stack of large cardboard boxes, towards which two of the men headed.

The others gathered around me. I ran my gaze over their inquisitive faces. There were Senka Veselinović and Stanislav Mirić, as well as four others. I had difficulty recognizing them too because they had all changed their appearance. They were all now clean cut and dressed like yuppies—the complete opposite of the look that I remembered from eight months earlier.

The burly young man no longer had short hair or sports clothes, and the tattoo on his left earlobe was gone. The small young lady with a mole on the tip of her nose had short light hair instead of long and dark, and she had lost a few pounds. The elegant suit made the greatest difference on the long-haired young man who had previously worn faded jeans and the brick-colored sweatshirt, with loosely-laced running shoes. It was also difficult to imagine that the round-faced girl, who looked the best in a business suit, until recently had unruly hair and went around with her bellybutton showing.

"I'm glad that we meet again, young colleagues," I said with a smile. "You've really scrubbed up nicely."

The two girls responded with brief skittish smiles.

"The Grand Master and his band, right?" Agent Mirić said.

"I'm certain about the Grand Master. If the band was present too, they didn't make a sound in the dark. Although there was some commotion, but that could have been the guard, Rabrenović, who brought me here."

"Why did he bring you?" Agent Veselinović asked.

"For a chat. A very useful one. First of all, I learned what is going on this time. After *The Last Book* and *The Grand Manuscript*, they are expecting *The Compendium of the Dead*: a set of four books that contain information about all the people who ever lived. Around a hundred billion of them."

The six agents silently exchanged quick glances.

"You mean the empty white books that you have been receiving since this morning? There are three of them, not four," Mirić noted.

"For now. The fourth should appear soon. The

books will then, allegedly, cease to be empty, although I didn't quite understand how so much data is to be stored in only four volumes. It is some sort of quantum recording."

Agent Mirić turned towards his colleague Veselinović.

"We have the report back from the lab," she said. "The source of the paper that was used to make the white books is unknown. No one produces it. Actually, it isn't even paper but rather some sort of foil. They're currently running tests on it."

"All right, let's say that someone puts all the data on foils," Mirić said. "Why does the secret society want *The Compendium of the Dead*?"

"Because," I responded, "they believe that whoever has the four-volume set will have the power to resurrect the dead."

Mirić watched me for several moments in silence, then rolled his eyes. "No less."

We were joined by the two men who had been inspecting the cardboard boxes. It was only when they came quite close that I realized it wasn't the first time I had encountered them either. I had seen them eight months ago, dressed in jeans and orange t-shirts, first going into 12 Oak Street, and then removing Inspector Vesić's corpse from there.

The taller of them shrugged as he looked at Agent Mirić.

"You will have a hard time figuring out how they disappeared," I said. "Even Commissioner Milenković was unsuccessful. They kept eluding him. I was present on one occasion when more than fifty of them vanished in around twenty seconds from a large chamber beneath a villa. They are very skilled at that."

"Skilled," said Agent Veselinović, "or capable of pulling off the impossible."

"There is no need for the impossible. They have obviously been interested in this building for a while, for some reason, if they had a man here. Probably even more than one. There was time to make a secret escape route in the attic, which isn't in use anyway. You can't expect to find it with a cursory inspection."

"Do you still think that they are behind everything that is happening today?"

"It seems the most likely thing to me."

"Then we have serious difficulties with at least one episode, the one at the Police Headquarters. We didn't give it just a cursory inspection, but a very thorough one. The disappearance and reappearance of Ms. Mirković cannot be explained."

"Did you consider the possibility that she is a member of the secret society? That would provide at least a partial explanation—we would know that she didn't stay in that car for only half a minute, as she claims."

"Even if we were to assume that, the main riddle remains unsolved—how did she first disappear from a moving elevator, and then reappear in it almost three hours later?"

"Patience. The answer to that may yet emerge."

Agent Mirić cleared his throat. "Did you tell the Grand Master that you think that he is pulling the strings?"

"I did. Of course, he denied it, but that doesn't mean anything. He would have denied it whether my assumption was correct or not: in the first case to protect himself, in the second to maintain my misconception. However, when I offered to give him the three copies that he allegedly cares about, he declined."

"Why did you offer him the books?"

"To do you a favor, in the name of our new cooperation. I asked that in return he reveal who is protecting them. This information, however, was more precious to him than *The Compendium of the Dead*, and the power that comes with it."

Agent Veselinović raised her hand to her right ear. Her eyes wandered away from me for a moment. She nodded twice without saying a word.

"We have another inexplicable episode," she said, lowering her hand. "The disappearance of Mr. Tripimirović from the locked Archive. Our experts have just determined that there is no other way out of the room. Perhaps the Grand Master was in fact being sincere when he denied that they were behind everything. Except, of course, if they are actually capable of performing the impossible."

"The archivist could have left the room, and then from the outside turned the key in the lock on the inside."

"The late Inspector Vesić told you that was impossible," Agent Mirić reminded me.

"That was in regard to a significantly more complex type of lock. The one downstairs is quite ordinary. I could probably pull that off."

"That might be the case, but it would be a tricky achievement for someone to whom the dip pen and inkwell are the pinnacle of technology."

"Perhaps someone more skillful helped him, if he too is a member of the secret society. . . ."

"You really are persistent, Inspector Lukić," Agent Veselinović interrupted. "You grasp at increasingly complicated explanations only to avoid the simplest one—that this a new case of crossing realities. It is as though you've completely forsaken Occam."

"Of course I haven't forsaken Occam. The only problem is that I don't think that crossing realities are the simplest explanation. On the contrary. By the way, you used the same words that the Grand Master and I exchanged when parting—'you really are persistent.'"

"There you have it."

"Why do you reject the possibility that realities have crossed again?" Agent Mirić asked. "I agree that it is not the simplest solution, but it is the only one that we have for the impossible. And there is a growing number of emerging impossibilities."

"I reject it because realities cross only when the author is writing a novel that is set in our world. A detective novel. It doesn't really matter that no one has been killed so far, and that such literary works don't exist without murder victims. Perhaps they will appear later, as you've said. What is crucial is that nothing that has happened so far looks like a detective novel. Not only is there no crime, but there isn't even anything that falls within the jurisdiction of the police. Someone is leaving for me, at different locations, empty white books, made of unusual paper. That is weird, I agree, but no laws were broken in the process. The lab technician disappeared in an elevator, then reappeared after a while. The circumstances are mysterious, but the girl is all right. Now the archivist has vanished. There are no signs of a struggle or any reason to suspect that something bad has happened. Why wouldn't he too return unscathed?"

I paused to catch my breath, only then realizing that I was speaking too quickly. Eight young faces were staring fixedly at me.

"If realities have crossed again," I continued, more slowly and softly, "if this truly is a detective novel, whoever is writing it is very unskilled in the art of writing."

Or very, very skilled, I thought to myself.

◈ 21 ◈

SENKA VESELINOVIĆ WAS ABOUT to say something, and it seemed that Stanislav Mirić also wanted to speak his mind, but they were forestalled by the ringing of my work cell phone. I held up my hand, asking them to wait, and took out my telephone. The chief inspector's name appeared on the screen.

"Inspector Lukić. How may I help you, Chief Inspector Uskoković?"

"Are you at Headquarters?"

"No, but I will be soon."

"Please come and see me as soon as you get here."

"Very well."

I returned the telephone to my pocket, then shrugged.

"I'm afraid we will have to resume our interesting discussion at another time." I smiled. "I have a feeling that it will be very soon."

"It looks like we will be seeing a lot each other today, Inspector Lukić," replied Agent Veselinović, also with a smile.

I left the attic and ran down the creaking wooden steps. As I headed down the second-floor corridor, two or three curious heads peered out of the doors that had been left ajar.

On the ground floor I ran into the crime scene team just as they were arriving. I showed them where to go. "People from the National Security Agency were there until a little while ago. They didn't find anything. Even so, check it again," I added.

My two colleagues, wearing white protective coveralls and carrying large duffel bags, nodded and headed towards the basement. On the staircase they passed the administrator, who was on her way up. Having run into me, she first looked me over in surprise, as though asking what I was still doing there.

"Hasn't the crime scene team already finished?" she asked, nodding downstairs.

"Yes, it has. These are reinforcements. This is not a simple case, as you are well aware. Has the locksmith arrived?"

"Not yet." She gave me a reproachful look. "People are very careless about time. Mr. Rosić is again standing guard at the Archive door." She paused. "The first team didn't find anything?"

"No, they didn't, but I have good news for you. You

won't have any more problems with Rabrenović, the guard. He has decided to take early retirement."

Mrs. Leleković glanced towards the guard's booth in confusion. I didn't wait for her to turn towards me and ask for an explanation; I quickly left the building, and after taking two steps down the gravel path I was already at the gate.

There was a surprise awaiting me on the car. Tucked beneath the left windshield wiper was a parking violation ticket. As I removed it I realized that it was actually two tickets. The second was for unauthorized use of an emergency light. The traffic warden obviously hadn't bothered to check whether it was an unmarked police car. I guessed that people often used unauthorized emergency lights around here, and he had simply assumed that this was the case. I shook my head, folded the two pieces of paper and placed them in my pocket. I removed the emergency light, got in the car and placed it in the glove compartment. Just as on the previous occasion, two drivers pounced on the place that I had vacated, without any consideration for the fact that it was illegal to park there.

As I set off down the street, it crossed my mind that since this affair had started this morning, it was only when driving that I had had the opportunity to think things through without any interruption. The rest of the time had passed nearly without let-up.

There was one weak link in what I had told the National Security Agency agents at the end. I had avoided taking a stance on the disappearance of Ms. Mirković, vaguely describing it as mysterious. Had they pressured me into being more specific, I would have had to agree that the episode was the strongest corroboration of their assumption that it was a new case of crossing realities.

What happened in the elevator at the Police Headquarters could only be explained by the interference of a higher power. And the only higher power in our world was the author who acted out of his own universe. His interventions, however, were not arbitrary. He had to take into account the coherence what he was writing. He could not just introduce an episode that made no sense, which is precisely what the event in the elevator seemed to be.

The girl should have disappeared in a more natural way, and then either not appear again or turn up dead somewhere. That would have been not only coherent but also in the spirit of detective novels. However, this way it remained unclear why he had resorted to a mysterious disappearance, only for her to return a while later, as though nothing had happened. It seemed that the episode was an end in itself. It was like something an inexperienced and up-and-coming author would write, only to flaunt his imaginativeness, without any concern for its purpose in the novel as a whole.

Unless, of course, this was a case of what had occurred to me at the end of that long monologue in the attic. What I had left unsaid. I knew for a fact that the author was not inexperienced. He would not have failed to notice such a big slip-up. Perhaps the episode made sense, only I could not see how because it was masterfully concealed, and I still didn't have the time to focus on figuring it out.

Caught up in thought, the drive to the Police Headquarters seemed to me quite short. The doors to both elevators in the garage were closed, which could mean that the right-hand one was back in service. I pressed the call button. A full minute passed before the left-hand car arrived. On the way up, the elevator stopped on the ground floor. Two colleagues and a young woman I didn't recognize got in. They were deep in conversation, but fell silent as soon as they saw me. The men just nodded to me briefly, and then again as they got off on the third floor.

Having reached the fourth floor, I headed left and knocked on the last door on the right. The inscription on the brass plate read "Chief Inspector." Although her official title was "Chief Inspectoress", she didn't like it and had left the plate unchanged.

I could barely hear the invitation to enter over the parrots' loud screeches. I didn't see them, however, when I went in. Chief Inspector Uskoković was in the middle of pulling a heavy cover over the large cage. Once she had lowered it all the way, the squawking stopped.

"They don't usually make so much noise when someone comes in," she said, returning to the massive desk. She kept it very tidy, but it seemed somehow bare without former Chief Inspector Đorđević's two bonsais.

"Have a seat, Inspector Lukić."

She indicated the right armchair in front of the desk. As I sat down, it crossed my mind that this was the first time I had been seated there. Her predecessor had always offered me the left one.

"First of all, I want to confirm to you what you already know: Ms. Mirković is all right. The doctor didn't find any . . . irregularity . . . and she feels fine. Let's hope that it stays that way."

"I saw her shortly after she . . . returned. She seemed all right to me too."

"In order for it to remain so, it would be best not to remind her of what she has been through. I would ask that you avoid talking to her about it. I recommended the same to Mr. Grubijanić. The two of you are the only ones fully informed of . . . the event."

I nodded.

"The investigation will be suspended. Officially—nothing happened. Ms. Mirković has a little amnesia, that's all."

I nodded again.

"Unofficially, as you are well aware, the case has been

taken over by the National Security Agency. The building is full of their people." She paused. "It seems to me that they are especially interested in you."

"Yes, we had a long talk in my office."

"About what, if it isn't a secret?"

"About three unusual books that I received during the morning. You saw one in the lab."

She watched me for several moments in silence.

"Your previous . . . special . . . cases also started with books, correct?"

"A book and a manuscript, to be precise."

"A book and a manuscript, yes. Is this the third such case?"

Now it was I who looked at her for a few seconds mutely.

"I don't know," I responded at last, shrugging my shoulders. "The Agency believes that it is, but I'm not sure. It could also be that someone else is behind everything."

"Who could pull off this thing with the elevator?"

"There is a rather powerful secret society. . . ."

"So powerful that it can perform miracles in the Police Headquarters?"

"So powerful that it seems that even the Agency can't do anything about it."

We looked at each other again without words.

"I would very much appreciate it, Inspector Lukić, if you would keep me informed about any further developments in the case. I hope that the Agency has not prohibited that."

"No, it hasn't. At least not yet."

"Very well." The chief inspector stood up. "Call me if you need any help."

"I will. Thank you."

I too got up and headed towards the door. Before reaching it, Chief Inspector Uskoković spoke again.

"I'm glad that you like Saramago."

I turned around and smiled.

As I walked away down the corridor, a muffled screeching resounded behind me. I climbed the stairs rapidly to the fifth floor. I reached for the doorknob, convinced that the two agents had left the office unlocked, but I was mistaken—they had thoughtfully locked up. As I pulled out the bunch of keys, I heard the rustling of the tickets that I had placed in my pocket.

Having entered, I placed the two pieces of paper on the desk. It was something that could be taken care of later. I returned the keys to my pocket, sank into the chair and sighed loudly. Finally, an opportunity to gather my thoughts.

However, it wasn't to be. A moment later my work cell phone rang. Shaking my head, I took it out. The name on the screen was Bumbaković.

"Mrs. Evgenija Ognjanović from the National Library is on the line for you."

"Put her through."

"Inspector Lukić?" The voice of the head of the Department of Old and Rare Books was on the verge of tears.

"What has happened, Mrs. Ognjanović?"

"Please come as quickly as possible."

"What has happened?" I repeated my question.

"I . . . I can't tell you over the telephone. Please, come."

"I'm on my way."

I didn't waste any time locking the office. There was no longer anything anyone was interested in, and a regular lock certainly wasn't a serious obstacle if someone really wanted to get in.

I reached the elevator in three strides and pressed the call button with unnecessary force. About half a minute later the doors of the right-hand car opened. I had already taken a step inside, when a sudden realization stopped me in my tracks.

Stepping back, I turned around and no less hastily returned to my office. It was unclear to me how I hadn't noticed immediately that which had twice been right in front of my nose: first where I had parked illegally in front of the City Cemeteries Administration Building, and then a little while ago when I had placed the parking tickets on the desk.

I grabbed the two crumpled papers from the desk.

~ 22 ~

I DIDN'T HAVE ANY of the envelopes to compare the handwriting, but I didn't need them. I remembered it well. There wasn't much text written in pen on the tickets, just a few words. However, it was enough. The same hand that had addressed the three envelopes to me had also filled out these two forms. At the bottom, in the space indicated for the signature, was an illegible initial.

Of course, it was pointless to call the Department of Transportation and inquire who had been on duty in the vicinity of the City Cemeteries Administration Building. The local traffic warden would know nothing about these papers. Also, there was no reason to take these tickets to my colleagues at the Department of Transportation to have them canceled. They had no record of them at all. Actually, there was nothing I could do about it.

I folded the papers and returned them to the pocket with the keys, then I hustled to the elevator. Fortunately, the right-hand car was still there, and I reached the garage without making any stops. I took out the emergency light and switched it on; I drove out into the street faster than usual, with tires screeching.

Whoever had written those tickets felt such superiority that he had decided to toy with me. It was no longer enough to bamboozle me by sending unusual books and performing disappearing acts. He was convinced that I could not find him, so it pleased him to play a joke on me. What other purpose could this move have?

Then it occurred to me that perhaps he hadn't gone unnoticed. The Agency surely had installed video surveillance at the City Cemeteries Administration Building and in its vicinity during the operation. It was routine procedure. I would call them up and ask that they check the footage. I was already reaching for the telephone when I realized that I didn't have the telephone numbers of Stanislav Mirić or Senka Veselinović, or anyone else from the Agency. My only contact with them was the former Commissioner. I still had Milenković's phone number, but it had undoubtedly been disconnected after he retired.

Perhaps, however, I didn't need the telephone at all. My car was most certainly bugged, despite our cooperation. Just in case. It would probably be enough to ask out loud for them to call me. Or not. I could get them into trouble, which wouldn't do anyone any good. Whatever the case, it was very likely that the footage would reveal nothing, just like the footage from in front of the Café Mocha eight months ago. The superior prankster, who had left the fake tickets, must have been aware that the Agency was recording, and would have made sure to execute everything without being detected.

Few people would be bold enough to amuse themselves so arrogantly. Actually such brazen insolence was typical of only one person's nature—that of the Grand Master. I strained to recall whether I had even seen anything that he had written in his own hand. Anything at all. Unfortunately, nothing came to mind. He must have been convinced that I hadn't, otherwise he would not so openly flaunt his handwriting.

If, however, it was the Grand Master and his secret society who were behind everything, then I was once again confronted with the question of how he could pull off the episode in the elevator at the Police Headquarters. They were very powerful, but they were not wizards. The impossible was not within their power.

I barely controlled myself sufficiently to avoid slowing the car down one more time as something else occurred to me. What if the idea of some force being "behind everything" were wrong? All my thoughts, both the conversations that I had had with the two agents, as well as the one with the Grand Master, had led me to the conclusion that someone from another reality was pulling the strings, controlling everything that was happening.

But that didn't necessarily have to be so. Perhaps there were in fact two separate series of events. What had happened at the Police Headquarters was impossible without crossing realities, fair enough; but nothing else required sorcery, not even the latest event—the disappearance of Mr. Trpimirović from the locked archive. This did in fact seem more like a magic trick, no more complex than the speedy escape of at least two people from a pitch-dark attic.

If the other events were being directed by the Grand Master—and it could be no one else—it was understandable that he wanted me to believe that these too were under the author's influence. The Grand Master had offered to withdraw immediately if I gave him the three books. He wanted to assure me that he had not sent them to me, but it was just a bluff. He knew that I could not give them to him because I did not have the volumes, and if I were to ask the Agency for them, they would certainly oppose my handing them over to him.

The idea of two independent narratives resolved many of the dilemmas, but not the main one: what was the meaning of everything that had transpired since the morning, and which was obviously still not over? How did *The Compendium of the Dead* fit into it?

THERE WERE NO FREE spaces in the parking lot behind the National Library, but the guard recognized my car as I was approaching and quickly opened the gate. He waved me to follow him and went towards a separate section on the left. He removed the metal sign reading "Reserved" and signaled me to park there.

"The director just left," he said after I had gotten out of the car. "He won't be coming back."

"Thank you," I said, with a small nod. It was obvious that he could barely contain his curiosity, so I hurried towards the staff entrance, to avoid giving him the opportunity to ask me anything.

The administrator was waiting for me behind the glass doors, just like Miss Šuvaković had that morning. She just said briskly "Follow me" and led me towards the elevator with her head bent. As we passed through the lobby, I turned towards the receptionist and smiled broadly at her. She too looked down, breaking off her obvious stare.

With a wavering hand Mrs. Ognjanović inserted the security key into the slot under the number "–3." As soon as the elevator started moving she began to weep. For several moments I didn't know what to do, then I went up to her and put my arm around her shoulders. She was so short that it felt like consoling a child.

"What has happened, Mrs. Ognjenović?" I asked softly.

She tried to answer, but had barely managed to get a word out when we reached the Department of Old and Rare Books. She had previously taken a handkerchief from her sleeve and dried her eyes and cheeks.

"Forgive me. This is too much for me." She paused. It looked as though she was about to cry again, but she controlled herself. "She's gone."

I looked around the Department. We were alone.

"Miss Šuvaković?" I asked.

She nodded.

"When did this happen?"

She looked at me for a moment as though she had not understood what I was asking. Then she collected herself.

"Shortly before I called you. I had gone upstairs briefly. A professor who had an appointment at three o'clock had arrived. We canceled all the others who were supposed to work here today. We didn't have his phone number. It was his first time here. Olivera usually greets and sees off all the visitors, but this time I asked to go. For decades I've been spending my workdays deep underground and never had a problem with it. However, after what had happened earlier, I felt confined. I decided to go up to the ground floor and apologize to the professor, just so that I could get out into the open."

"I admire you. I would definitely not be able spend all my time in the underworld."

"I thought so too in the beginning, but you get used to it. You even learn to love the underworld—as you call it. Nonetheless, the professor was waiting for me by the elevator. We spoke briefly, no longer than five or six minutes. He was considerate and expressed understanding for the extraordinary circumstances, even though, of course, I did not tell him what had happened."

"The elevator was open the entire time?"

"No, but it stayed on the ground floor. I would have heard if it had moved. In any case, when I pressed the button, the doors opened straight away."

"You didn't want to stay upstairs any longer? Perhaps go outdoors?"

She shook her head. "No. That was enough. I hurried back so that Olivera would not be alone. It was as though I had sensed something. . . ." She paused briefly. "When I came out, there was no one here. The

Department was empty. Olivera had disappeared. I immediately called you. . . ."

Her eyes filled again.

I scanned the large room once more.

"You didn't think that Miss Šuvaković had perhaps gone to the restroom?"

"She couldn't have. The restrooms are one level up, and you can only get there by elevator."

"That's not exactly convenient if a person is in a hurry, and the elevator is occupied."

She gave me a serious look. "We've never had such issues."

"Very well, if your deputy could not have used the elevator, as far as I understand, there is only one other way she could have gotten out—the emergency exit."

The administrator fiercely shook her head. "Out of the question."

I waited for her to say something more, but she just kept on staring at me.

"This time you will have to disclose more about this exit, if you want me to try and determine what has happened to Miss Šuvaković."

She shook her head somewhat less vigorously this time. "I . . . am not authorized. Please, you have to understand. . . ."

"In that case the only thing I can do is conclude that your colleague mysteriously vanished into thin air—and close the case. That wouldn't be unusual—about ten percent of missing persons disappear without a trace. As though they had fallen off the face of the earth."

"Oh, God! You don't know what you are asking of me. Only a handful of us know about it and it has to remain so. If it were to get out. . . ."

"You can be at ease. I'm a police inspector, and I absolutely understand the importance of this secret. I assure you that no one will learn it from me."

Looking away, she started to fold her arms. It was a good half-minute before her inner struggle was over.

"Stay here and face the elevator doors. You must not turn around under any circumstances until I call you. Under any circumstances. Do you understand?"

"I do."

By her barely audible steps I could tell that she had gone to the right of where I was standing. I didn't turn around; I wasn't interested in what she wanted to conceal—how the emergency exit was opened. There was a brief silence, and then a soft mechanical noise reached my ears.

"Inspector Lukić," Mrs. Ognjanović called out to me.

I turned around. She was standing alongside the left-hand wall, in the middle. A part of the bookcase, around two meters high, had moved inward, like an open door with a metal outer surface. As I approached, the administrator stepped into the darkness, from which a moment later came the sound of a switch being flipped.

"Here you are," she said after coming out. The motion of her hand towards the opening seemed to express capitulation.

∽ 24 ∾

I paused in front of the entrance, looking at the illuminated interior. The square space was no larger than an elevator shaft. It was almost completely filled by an iron spiral staircase of the same dark gray color as the unplastered concrete walls. A round post extended through the center of it like an axle.

I stuck my head in and looked up. My view was somewhat obstructed, so I couldn't judge how far up the spiral extended, but it had to be high.

"Where does it lead?"

"To the room with the safes on the second floor."

"I'd like to climb up, if you don't mind."

She nodded.

I went in and looked up once again, then stepped up next to the handrail on the left-hand side, because that was where the steps were widest. As soon as I started climbing the automatic counter in my head went on. The ascent was tedious. Every three revolutions there would be a pair of lights on the walls opposite each other. There were no landings or level markers. The ascent ended after a hundred and thirty-seven steps. Breathing with slight difficulty, I reached a small platform with a railing and a low metal ceiling.

A steel door stood in front of me. A key ring with a key hung on a hook next to the doorpost. I looked around, but there was nothing else to see. I started back down, my eyes fixed on my feet. I didn't feel it as much on the way up, but I was getting lightheaded from the constant spinning, so I grabbed the handrail. When I emerged from the shaft I felt a tightness in my calves.

"Please stand near the elevator and turn away again," said the administrator, as soon as I stepped into the large room.

I moved complacently enough, but stopped before reaching the elevator. Something wasn't right, although I couldn't quite put my finger on it. Then a realization broke through to the surface of my consciousness— on the way down my counter had reached a hundred and thirty-six. It took quite significant willpower not to turn around and glance suspiciously at the stairway, but to continue on as I had been instructed.

"Has there ever been reason to use the emergency exit?" I asked with my back to Mrs. Ognjanović.

Once again I heard the mechanical noise as the secret door on the left-hand wall started to close, but I didn't notice the administrator walk over to me. She was already standing by my side when she answered.

"No, there hasn't, but twice a year we have drills. We rehearse leaving that way. I dread it. It hasn't been easy for me to clamber up those stairs for some time now."

I turned around. "Why did you say that it was out of the question that Miss Šuvaković had left that way?"

"First of all, because it's not allowed. There are strict rules on when that exit may be used. Only in the event of a natural disaster or war, and even then there is a complex protocol."

"People don't exactly always stick to what has been strictly prescribed. . . ."

She shook her head. "You don't know Olivera; the future administrator of this department considers the rules to be sacred."

"We still have to assume that she broke them for some reason. As far as I can see, the only way that she could have left is by way of that staircase." I pointed in the direction of the secret door.

"Impossible, Inspector. Had anyone appeared upstairs, in the room with the safes, I would have immediately been notified. There are always two people on duty there. Nonetheless, more importantly, my deputy is not allowed to leave the Department while I am out. At least one of us must be here during office hours. Olivera would never break that rule."

I looked around the large library, then shrugged my shoulders.

"If that is so, then we are confronted with an unsolvable puzzle. Miss Šuvaković's disappearance seems impossible, yet she is gone. Furthermore, this is not the first impossibility that has occurred here today: we still don't know how the two books appeared."

"So it was in fact only a book in the envelope? Nothing more dangerous than that?"

"Just a book," I responded with some hesitation.

"Also an old edition. . . ."

"No, quite new. Nothing that would be of interest to you."

"Why did they send it to you here?"

"I have no idea. Another puzzle. Incidentally, speaking of books, I'd like to leaf through the incunabulum, if you would permit me to. Not with my bare hands, of course." I pulled out plastic gloves from my inner pocket and started putting them on. "It is unlikely that I will ever have another opportunity."

She studied me for several moments without saying anything.

"Face the wall again," she said finally.

I complied for the third time. Now I couldn't determine by her footsteps where she had headed, but judging by the time it took her—I would say that she had almost reached the opposite end of the room. There was a brief silence, then the administrator spoke up in a changed tone.

"Inspector Lukić. . . ."

I turned around and saw her standing to the left of the furthest bookcase. She was looking down. I hurried towards her.

Nearly at the bottom of the bookcase a small drawer was pulled out. Empty.

"It's gone. The incunabulum has disappeared," Mrs. Ognjanović said almost in a whisper.

"Are you sure that you placed it here? Perhaps it's in another bookcase."

She shook her head. "This is the only one that has a secret drawer." She leaned over, touching the inside, as though she didn't believe her eyes, then she pushed it back. When it was in all the way, there was no visible sign that it was there. It obviously no longer mattered that I too knew its location.

"Did Miss Šuvaković know where you had hidden the incunabulum?"

"She was the one who put it there. Why do you ask?"

"I'm just checking," I responded while taking off the gloves.

"You don't mean to say. . . ."

"I mean to say," I interrupted her, "that now in addition to the mysteriously missing person we also have a mysteriously missing precious book, and that is more than enough reason to launch an investigation."

The administrator started speaking very quickly. "That must be avoided at all costs! We've explained to you. The reputation of our Department. . . ."

"I'm sorry, but I have to abide by the regulations. I'm sure you understand. In any case, I will do my best to act as discreetly as possible, as I promised."

"Oh, my god. . . ." she muttered and clutched her head.

"Of course, an investigation would not be necessary if by some miracle both your deputy and the incunabulum were to appear. The Department would be spared the unpleasantness."

I waited a little while for a response, but Mrs. Ognjanović just kept looking at me while holding her head.

"All right, I have to go now. I hope that you will call me soon with good news."

∽ 25 ∾

STEPPING INTO THE ELEVATOR, I was about to touch the button marked zero, when the call of nature, which I had been feeling for some time, reminded me that the administrator had said that the nearest facility that I required was above the Department of Old and Rare Books. My finger slipped down to the "–3" button.

After the short ride, I proceeded down a well lit corridor, which after about fifteen meters turned sharp right. I didn't know what was located here, but it seemed as lavish as the lower level. The walls were covered in reddish marble panels, and thick carpeting of the same color covered the stone floor. Along both sides, at regular intervals, were padded doors without any nameplates. There was no one in sight, nor were there any sounds.

I finally found the restrooms just before the turn—first the women's then the men's. The inside was even more luxurious than the corridor: marble also covered the ceiling, a huge mirror filled the upper half of the wall above the porcelain sinks; there was even a shower, and the shelf next to it was stacked with towels and various personal hygiene and grooming supplies.

Feeling slightly like an intruder in this place—which was not intended for ordinary visitors to the National Library, including police inspectors—I entered the nearest stall. As soon as I had closed the door the sweet scent of air freshener arose, accompanied by soft music.

The circumstances were quite inappropriate, but the peace around me brought me the focus that I had managed to achieve today only when I was alone in the car. Actually, here it was a bit more favorable to contemplation since I did not also have to focus on driving. There were no distractions.

There were two possible explanations for the seemingly impossible disappearance of Miss Šuvaković.

The first was that she wasn't missing at all, but was still hidden somewhere in the Department of Old and Rare Books. Perhaps there was another secret exit or hiding place behind the bookshelves that I was not aware of; perhaps she had sought refuge in one of the large bookcases, taking the incunabulum with her. The administrator claimed that the small drawer, in which the ancient book had allegedly been placed, was the only secret compartment, but I had no reason to believe her.

The second was that I also didn't have to believe the administrator's claim that her deputy had stayed in the Department while she went to the ground floor to meet with the professor. They could have left together, and Miss Šuvaković could have gotten off at one of the underground levels, carrying the incunabulum. The National Library doubtless had good security camera coverage, but anyone aware of their placement would know how to evade them.

In both cases, the administrator and her deputy would have been in cahoots, with the aim of achieving something. Two options presented themselves here too, depending on whether the two of them were members of the Grand Master's band or not.

If they were members, then the purpose of removing the incunabulum would be to deny me the opportunity to verify whether it truly was a second copy of *The Book of Resurrection*, as I had been told. The question here would be why it had been felt necessary to bring the false incunabulum to the Department, along with the envelope addressed to me, when the same result could have been achieved without it. The answer might be that it was in order to present everything to me as being foggier and more mysterious,.

The pattern from the City Cemeteries Administration had been replicated. In that case the books had first been moved around, mimicking the patient from the Papyrus, only for the archivist, along with two books of burial records, to disappear in the end, even though it was unnecessary. Here someone had brought the book in first, copying a different patient from the Papyrus, only for the deputy to disappear later, along with *The Book of Resurrection*, which didn't need to appear at all in the first place.

Even if this was true, however, I was still no closer to solving the main puzzle—why was the secret society leaving me the volumes of *The Compendium of the Dead* and why was it denying that it was doing so?

On the other hand, if the two women had no connection to the Grand Master, as he himself claimed, then it must be a real incunabulum, which the two of them were trying to steal, forsaking the high ideals of which they were so proud. We would see whether they would accept my closing offer—that I would stop the investigation if the book was returned.

Though, in this case again, the main puzzle remained unsolved—how did the second copy of *The Book of Resurrection*, along with the second volume of *The Compendium of the Dead*, appear at the Department?

Even though I was still surrounded by puzzles, after careful contemplation I came out of the stall feeling relieved. I walked up to the first sink and washed my hands, pleased that no one had come in, so I didn't have to come up with an explanation as to what I was doing there. I dried my hands in the almost noiseless stream of warm air and walked towards the door.

∽ 26 ∾

THE CORRIDOR WAS STILL deserted. It crossed my mind at that moment that this might not be an active department, but rather a shelter for the Library staff in the event of an emergency. A little luxury wouldn't hurt if one were forced to stay here for an extended period. I would have expected the deepest level to be chosen for housing people, but the dedicated librarians had the final say, and they didn't hesitate to put the safety of the old and rare books ahead of their own. The two ladies who worked downstairs and their refined visitors had a private restroom at their disposal, which was fitting. Perhaps they would have minded if they'd known that I had used it.

I had already reached the elevator when it occurred to me that something was not right. I turned around and looked down the corridor. Everything seemed the same as when I had come in, but I could not shake the feeling that something was off. I stood there for several moments, than headed back, while looking around, although there wasn't much to see. I was about halfway down the corridor when I finally realized what it was.

Attached to the frame of the door in front of which I had stopped, was an oval brass plate that had not been there earlier. I could trust my memory: I certainly had not overlooked it. Previously there had been nothing interrupting the upper portion of the wooden frame. I looked around and checked the doors that I had already passed, and then the ones in front of me. Of the ten of them eight now had such plates—five on the left and three on the right. The plates on the two remaining right-hand doors were plastic and depicted a woman's and a man's shoe; they were the only ones that had been there when I had passed down the corridor the first time.

I returned to the elevator, then moved slowly from one door to the next, looking at the plates. They all had eight-digit numbers. These didn't mean anything to me. At first glance they were not special nor was there any progression, expect that they started with the same two digits: one and nine. Having reached the end, I took out my cell phone and started taking pictures of them. I could analyze them later.

I had been in the restroom for no more than ten minutes, but that was long enough to install these plates. There were no visible screws, which meant that they were glued on. I could try to remove one or all of them, but I had no reason to do so.

Had it been any other situation, I would not completely dismiss the highly unlikely possibility that during the precise time that I was in the restroom, members of the National Library maintenance staff had installed the plates in this part of the third underground level, with these very unusual inscriptions. However, today such a coincidence was out of the question. Only the members of the secret society could be behind this.

I had no clue what they wanted to achieve. They obviously had access even to restricted areas of the National Library, regardless of whether it was with the help of the administrator and her deputy, or unrelated to them. They were following me, so they had taken advantage of my time in the restroom to leave me this message, the meaning of which eluded me completely.

I pressed the elevator call button. The doors opened immediately, but this didn't mean that the car had been here the entire time since my arrival from the lower level. The Grand Master's people could have called it from somewhere, taken it to this level, finished the job, then retreated, sending back the empty elevator. If this was not the case, then they had arrived in another elevator. There was certainly more than one leading to the shelter.

I had no more reason to stay here, so I entered the car and pressed the zero button. As the doors closed I glanced at the corridor one more time. There were no more changes. When the two halves of the door parted soon after at the ground floor, I faced a welcome committee. In addition to Senka Veselinović and Stanislav Mirić, there were also the girl with the mole on the tip of her nose and the young man who had had a tattooed ear.

◇ 27 ◇

"YOU WERE DOWN THERE for quite a while, Inspector Lukić," said Mirić. "We were starting to get worried."

"You could have come down to see what was going on."

"We would have done very soon, had you not appeared," said Agent Veselinović.

"Luckily, I wasn't in any trouble, because if I had been, how could I call for help? It's questionable whether there is any cell coverage four levels underground, and even if there is—I don't know your phone numbers."

"We can fix that immediately." Mirić took his telephone out and with his thumb started typing on the small keypad. A moment later there was a ring in my pocket. "There, you now have my number. Although you didn't really need it. We would have been in contact even if you had called someone else."

"Ah, yes. How could I forget that? Eavesdropping in the spirit of true cooperation."

"Would I have told you if it was eavesdropping? We're only keeping an open line with you so that we can come to your aid if need be. Precisely in the spirit of true cooperation."

"By the way," the girl spoke again, "the underground levels of the National Library are equipped with microrelays. Network coverage is as good as it is above ground."

"That won't be of any use to me. I don't think I'll have any more business at the Department of Old and Rare Books."

"How is that?" Mirić asked. "Nothing has been resolved here, quite the contrary. Everything has become more complicated with the disappearance of Miss Šuvaković and the incunabulum."

I thought of asking how he knew all that. Mrs. Ognjanović hadn't told anyone except me. But I had just been given the answer. The microrelays obviously had another purpose, besides ensuring cell phone coverage.

"Her disappearance is the conclusion of the second act in a performance being put on by the secret society. They did the same at the City Cemeteries Administration. The main purpose was to deliver these books to me. The rest is there to create the illusion of mystery."

"The illusion is outstanding. Like the archivist, the deputy seems actually to have magically disappeared. We have the National Library under tight surveillance. She did not leave the building. She is actually in the Department of Old and Rare Books."

"Then search it and you will find her. And the false incunabulum too."

Agent Mirić stared at me for several moments.

"We checked all the places where she could hide. She's not there. And there is no incunabulum, genuine or fake."

It was pointless to ask how they had checked it without being detected, or how they even knew about all the places. He most likely would not have told me, despite the unreserved cooperation between us.

"We're going around in circles," I said. "You are still underestimating the Grand Master, and he feels so superior that he is toying with us." I took out the two pieces of paper from my pocket and handed them to Mirić. "This is what he placed under the windshield wipers of my car while we were at the City Cemeteries Administration. There's no need to check the cameras—you won't see anything."

The other three gathered around Mirić and gazed at the supposed tickets.

"The handwriting is the same as that on the envelopes," said the girl with the mole.

I nodded. "That's right. It seems that even that wasn't enough, so he continued his toying just now. While I was in the restroom on the third underground level, his people placed brass plates with numbers on the surrounding doors. I suspect that they did this to send me on a wild goose chase to make some sense of them. You can try for yourselves if you want—the plates are still down there."

Mirić nodded to the other pair without a word and they headed to the elevator, which was still at the ground floor.

"So, that's what kept you," said Agent Veselinović. "I was just wondering. . . ."

"I don't know what it's like for secret agents, but ordinary police inspectors occasionally have the need to visit the restroom."

"I'd like to take this for the moment, if you have no objections," said Mirić, holding up the two pieces of paper.

"Be my guest. Do you perhaps have a sample of the Grand Master's handwriting somewhere on file?"

"I don't know. I would have to check. However, let's assume that you are right and that he is the person pulling the strings. There's one thing I don't understand. Why would he send you the books that he himself is so interested in?"

I shrugged. "I have no idea. There is surely some reason. And I guess it will have to be revealed when he finally delivers the last, fourth volume to me."

I expected them to respond to this, but no one said a word. We spent about two minutes in silence. Once I glanced at the otherwise curious receptionist. She kept her head down. It looked like she didn't dare raise her eyes in our direction.

The silence was interrupted by the elevator doors opening. The young woman and man came out of the cabin.

"There are no plates above the doors in the corridor," she said, shaking her head.

"So they removed them after I left," I said. "It doesn't matter. I took pictures of them."

I took out my cell phone and flipped through the menus. When the first photo appeared on the screen it took great effort for me to keep a steady face. I was saved from my predicament by a sudden ringing. I removed the picture with a quick swipe and answered the call.

∽ 28 ∽

"GVOZDEN VIDOJEVIĆ IS CALLING for you again," Bumbaković said to me. "He says it's urgent. He sounds upset."

"Patch me through."

"Inspector Lukić?" said the old poet in a trembling voice.

"Yes, Mr. Vidojević."

"My Sofija . . . She's gone."

Under different circumstances I would probably have asked a question; the way things were I just responded "I'll be right there." I put the phone back in my pocket, then turned to the agents. "As you've heard"—I pointed to their barely visible earpieces—"we have another disappearance: Mrs. Sofija Vidojević, the disabled wife of the man who received the third volume of *The Compendium of the Dead.*"

"A new illusion of mystery?" Mirić said calmly, without irony.

"We'll see," I responded, then hurried towards the glass door.

"Send us the pictures of the plates," Agent Veselinović shouted after me.

Without stopping, I turned and nodded.

I left the National Library and went to the car. There were now more free parking spaces around. I sat behind the wheel and took out my cell phone. I was in a hurry to see Mr. Vidojević, but this took precedence. Before anything else, I had to see the other seven photos taken in the corridor on the third underground level. It would only take a few seconds.

The pictures passed quickly because it was easy to make out what I was interested in. The change was significant: the numbers had been halved. Instead of the eight digits I had seen with my own eyes, the phone camera had captured four-digit numbers. At first glance, I would say that it was the second half that was lost, because the numbers still started with "19."

I paused briefly at the last photo, then entered the instructions for all eight of them to be sent to Agent Mirić's cell phone. I put the phone back in my pocket, started the engine and drove to the parking exit. The guard was standing by the ramp. As I passed by him he grinned from ear to ear and gave me a military-style salute.

Regardless of how skillful the Grand Master was at creating illusions, he could not have been behind this. Perhaps through hypnosis he could make me believe that I was seeing something that was not there, but when had he the opportunity to hypnotize me? There was not a living soul in the corridor or the restroom, and in the attic of the City Cemeteries Administration Building, which was the only place where we had met today, we were in the dark the entire time. I guessed it wasn't feasible to hypnotize someone in the dark.

No, what had happened above the Department of Old and Rare Books was not possible. And the impossible could be pulled off only by someone who influences our reality from another reality. I finally had to accept what I alone had stubbornly dismissed this morning, when everything had started—that realities were crossing again, and that in the other one someone was once again writing a novel that was set in our reality.

I should have realized this right after the first very obvious impossibility—the episode in the elevator at the Police Headquarters—but all this time I had been trying to explain it away. Quite rightly, I had been criticized for my stubbornness. I had been even more persistent in my attempts to convince the Grand Master that it was he who had been organizing the intricate performances in order to deliver the unusual books to me, even though it was simpler to assume that these, too, displayed signs of interference by the author.

Until now I had hesitated to accept that these were once again his actions, primarily because the purpose of them eluded me. It was the same this time. Why would he suddenly decide to make it clear to me that he was pulling the strings?

That was, presumably, the purpose of this game involving the disappearing digits in the photos. Or perhaps not? That is to say—perhaps it wasn't only that. What else could it be? I couldn't know until I had the chance to take a closer look a the numbers. If there was any meaning whatsoever, that was the only place where it could be concealed.

My conscience pricked me for betraying the young people from the National Security Agency. They had been fair to me. I should let them know that the photos I had sent them did not correspond to what I had seen on the plates. Very well, I told myself, I won't keep it from them. I'll just delay telling them for a little while, until I get a chance to look into the matter. Soon, I hope.

∽ 29 ∽

Once again there were no empty parking spaces in front of 14 Oak Street, so as before, I left the car in the parking lot of the adjacent building. In the upper left corner, the first and fourth windows were now open. An old lady had just made her way up to the glass front door, leading a white poodle on a leash.

In Mr. Vidojević's building I was once again greeted by semi-darkness and the same acid odor. I ran up the stairs and rang the old-fashioned doorbell. An eye instantly appeared in the large peephole, as though the old poet had been standing right next to the door. He still had on his dark red robe, bow tie and worn-out leather slippers.

"Come in, Inspector Lukić."

As he stepped back to let me through, he tried to smile, but it came out as a grimace. He closed the door behind me and led me down the corridor. The shelves, which completely covered the walls, were packed with books. The only illumination came from a weak light bulb which hung from the middle of the high ceiling. The air was dry and dusty, with a prevailing odor of stale paper.

At the end of the corridor we turned left into the study. Here, too, shelves full of books covered all the walls. The few pieces of furniture were pushed towards the center of the room: a desk buried in a disarray of papers, books and magazines, a worn-out dark red plush love seat, a matching armchair, a chair that seemed very flimsy. The blinds were lowered at an angle on both windows, and the soft light was provided by a desk lamp with a green shade, and a floor lamp in the opposite corner with a yellow one.

"Please," said Mr. Vidojević, indicating the armchair.

I settled down in it. For a moment he seemed to have doubts as to where to sit, then he took the other chair, which made a cracking noise.

"What happened?" I asked.

He shrugged and shook his head.

"I don't know . . . I don't understand. . . ."

"Tell me everything that you know."

"Someone rang the bell. Sofija and I were here. I was at the desk, she over there—in her wheelchair." He pointed towards the left-hand window. "She likes to sit there, although she won't let me raise the blinds. . . ." He fell silent for a moment. "I went to see who it was. I looked through the peephole—there was no one. I thought that it might be kids; they sometimes ring the bell and run away. I was on my way back, when I heard the doorbell again. I immediately opened the door. Again—no one. I looked down the stairwell—everything was deserted. I was about to close the door, when I noticed two copies of *Small Poems of Death* on the doormat. You can imagine how delighted I was—three books in one day."

He looked at me as though expecting me to respond. I nodded.

"I have received deliveries like this before," he continued. "People know what I collect. When they come across the book somewhere, they buy it and bring it to me, but they won't give it to me in person. As I've told you—they don't want any reward. In most cases they place the books in the mailbox. On two occasions they left them on the doorstep, like today. Once they rang the bell and quickly went off, the second time they just left it. I brought the books inside to show them to Sofija. She was also very glad. Then I went to the cellar to put them away. When I came back. . . ."

His voice trembled, then he fell silent. Not wanting to rush him, I waited for him to pull himself together.

"When I came back, Sofija was gone. I first thought that she had gone to a different room. In the wheelchair she moves around the apartment with ease. Outside I always push her. But she was nowhere to be found. I looked everywhere, the apartment isn't big. . . ."

"Did you lock the door before going to the basement?"

"No, I didn't. I never do. That would be insulting to Sofija."

"There's something I don't understand. . . ." I paused. "How long has Mrs. Vidojević been in the wheelchair?"

"Since the publication of *Small Poems of Death*. She didn't only stop speaking, but also stopped using her legs."

"So, medically there are no problems with her legs, she just refuses to use them?" I asked.

He looked at me for several moments without speaking.

"What are you trying to say?"

"I'm trying to establish whether she was capable of leaving here on her own, while you were absent."

"Physically she is, but she would never do that. You don't know Sofija. She wouldn't get up and walk even if the apartment was on fire and I was out, and there was no one else to come to her rescue."

"Perhaps there is something that she considers worse than death by fire, something that would make her change her mind."

"What could that be? As you can see, everything is normal here, except that Sofija is gone. And I was in the cellar for no more than five or six minutes."

"It didn't have to be something external. Perhaps it was something within her. Mrs. Vidojević is obviously a woman with a very . . . particular . . . personality."

The old poet shook his head.

"You're on the wrong track, Inspector. Sofija truly is an exceptional woman—would she have been my muse my entire life otherwise? But she did not leave here on her own two feet. If she had, why would she have taken the wheelchair with her? It is also gone."

Of course, I should have noticed that, but somehow I had overlooked it.

"All right, so what do you think happened?"

"Someone took Sofija away in the wheelchair. They brought me the books to lure me out of the apartment. They knew that I would take them to the cellar straight away. They used my absence to get their hands on Sofija." His voice fluttered once again. "I only hope that they didn't hurt her in order to subdue her. Had she resisted while being taken out, I would have heard it from the cellar. I had left the main door open. But everything was quiet. . . ."

"If it is a kidnapping, as you believe, then we must first try to figure out why she was abducted. I have to ask you—are you wealthy? Perhaps the kidnappers are hoping for a ransom."

"My dear Inspector, you of all people know about literature. Have you ever heard of a wealthy poet? Everything anyone could hope for from me are these books here." He smiled sourly. "And the ones in the cellar. And no one would resort to kidnapping for that."

"Is there anyone who wants to harm you? Are you

at odds with anyone? After greed, revenge is the most common reason for abduction."

He shook his head. "I've never clashed with anyone. No one has reason to seek revenge against me."

"What else could it be? Do you have any suspicions?"

He looked at me silently for several moments. When he spoke again his voice was softer.

"Envy."

I thought I hadn't heard him well. "Excuse me?"

"Envy. They envy me because of Sofija."

"Who?" I asked confusedly.

"Other poets. Each and every one of them. No one has such a muse."

Now it was I who was without words for a few moments.

"Did any of them ever say anything to that effect?"

"They didn't have to. I know. Poets are very, very envious."

"All right, perhaps they envy you, but that would hardly give cause for abduction. At least I have not heard of such a case in criminology. And if my memory serves me, there are no instances in the history of literature of muses being abducted out of envy, either."

"So why then would someone kidnap Sofija?" The old man's face seemed to shatter into a dozen pieces. He was on the verge of breaking down in tears.

"We should know that very soon."

"Soon?"

"Yes. Kidnappers usually call after a short while to state their demands. Until then we can't do much. Stay here and wait for their call, then inform me immediately. Don't do anything on your own."

I got up out of the armchair, as did Mr. Vidojčvić from his chair, which made a cracking noise again.

"Do you think they will . . . harm . . . my Sofija?"

I shook my head. "They won't, don't worry. They wouldn't be able to achieve their aim that way. In any case—who would dare harm a muse?"

I went into the corridor. The old poet followed me. I was already at the front door when he spoke again.

"How is you investigation going, Inspector?"

"Investigation?"

"You know, the envelope with your name on it. Did you find out why it was left in my cellar?"

"I haven't yet, but I'm working on it. It should be cleared up soon too."

∽ 30 ∾

JUST AS EIGHT MONTHS earlier, I felt a brief weakness as I approached the parking lot in front of 12 Oak Street. The ensuing rumble in my stomach reminded me that I hadn't eaten anything since the morning. Events had followed one after another, without giving me the chance to catch my breath. I looked at my wristwatch—seventeen minutes to five. I hadn't realized it was already so late.

I unlocked the door and settled down in the seat. Usually at the end of the day I stop by the office. There are always some technical tasks that need to be attended to. Today I could skip it and go straight home, but I still headed down to the Police Headquarters. I wouldn't stay long; I had promised Ms. Mirković that I would pop in. I also wanted to take a look at the pictures of the numbered plates from the National Library, and the archives, which I couldn't access remotely, could be useful for that.

If the disappearance of Mrs. Vidojević had been a regular case, there would have been a simple solution: the eccentric lady had simply wanted to go for a walk, and because she was obstinate she didn't just go out, which would have been simplest, but she also quietly carried the wheelchair down to the street, so that her husband wouldn't hear her through the open basement door. She had then ridden in it somewhere, or pushed it empty. This would have been quite typical for a muse who had suddenly decided not to speak or walk until her poor husband collected up all the copies of his poetry collection, which for who knows what reason she had suddenly found displeasing.

This, however, could not be a regular case because the envelope with my name on it, which had been left in the cellar, did not fit anywhere.

If it was part of the performance by the Grand Master, the disappearance of the muse would have been devised primarily to confuse me; I would struggle to find some connection between the delivery of the third volume of *The Compendium of the Dead* and her alleged kidnapping. My search would be impeded by the excellent actor playing the role of Mr. Vidojević. He seemed very convincing as the poet completely spellbound by his capricious wife.

This too, however, was not possible. Again the envelope did not fit anywhere. The Grand Master did not have any reason to leave it for me, since he himself was also trying to get his hands on what was in it. The first volume had gotten away from him, by his own admission, because the guard, Rabrenović, was not wakeful enough. The second one had appeared in a place that was highly inaccessible, even for his secret society. The third one, however, would have been within his reach had the actor in the role of Mr. Vidojević been his man.

The envelopes did not create problems only if they had been sent by the author. The mysterious books in them were intended for me—and they had reached me. Albeit, they did not remain in my possession, but that wasn't important at the moment. This, however, raised a number of other questions: Why was I getting the books? If there were actually supposed to be four of them, as the Grand Master claimed, where was the last one? What was the purpose of the other events that had accompanied the appearance of the books? All three in-

cidents had ended with a mysterious disappearance—
first Mr. Trpimirović, the archivist, then Miss Šuvaković, the Deputy Administrator of the Department
of Old and Rare Books, and finally Mrs. Vidojević, the
poet's wife. How did these people disappear? Where
were they now? What were these episodes supposed to
achieve?

And finally, the most difficult of all questions: what
was the sense of the totality, of everything that had
happened since the morning? What kind of a novel was
the author writing?

There was no time to dive into these questions
because I had just entered the garage at the Police
Headquarters. At this hour there were numerous free
spaces, so I parked the car quite near the elevator and
the entrance to the basement section of the building.
Stepping into the corridor I looked at my watch: eight
minutes to five. I knocked on the door to the lab and
entered.

Inside I came across two female and one male lab
technicians. They were getting ready to call it a day. All
three of them looked at me curiously.

"Is Ms. Mirković still here?" I asked.

"No, she isn't," answered the younger of the two
ladies, a slender dark-haired woman with thick eyebrows. "She just went home. She left a message for you.
She said she would see you later."

I looked at her confusedly. "When later?"

The technician shrugged, as though apologizing. "I
don't know, Inspector."

∽ 31 ∽

IT WAS ONLY AFTER exiting the car on the fifth floor
that I realized I had not paid attention to which elevator I was getting into in the garage. I rode the left one,
but hopefully that no longer mattered. The author was

unlikely to play with the elevator anymore. He would only be repeating himself, and that is not a mark of good writing. Regardless of the type of detective novel he had come up with this time, above all he would still have to make sure that the writing was good.

I was already reaching into my pocket to retrieve the office key, when I remembered that in my haste I had not locked the door. I entered, sat down at the desk and turned on the computer. While waiting for the system to boot up, I looked around the room. The rays of the low sun filled it with a soft light. Everything appeared as usual.

I took out my cell phone and transferred the eight photos from the third underground level of the National Library to the hard drive, and then on the big screen I studied the images of the brass plates. I could not determine whether the phone's camera had seen slightly smaller plates than I had, or perhaps their size was the same, while the illusion that they were smaller was because the digits on them were larger. In any case, there was no indication that any of the digits were missing; there was exactly space for four digits on the plates.

I didn't have to look at the images for very long; there were no details that I could examine. The only thing left was to analyze the numbers more carefully. I opened a text editor and copied the eight four-digit numbers in the order in which I had taken the pictures.

The numbers on the list generated this way were jumbled: 1948, 1950, 1993, 1964, 1980, 1977, 1973 and 1961. I tried to work out some pattern, but didn't learn anything except that there were four even and four odd numbers. Next I split them into two unequal groups—the five numbers that were above the doors on the left side (1950, 1964, 1977, 1973 and 1961), and the three from the right side (1948, 1993 and 1980), but no sense appeared there either.

Then I arranged them in ascending order: 1948,

1950, 1961, 1964, 1973, 1977, 1980 and 1993. I stared at the monitor for a while, trying to make out any mathematical coherence. This was not a sequence of primes—that was obvious at first glance—nor any other sequence that I was aware of, although there were not many of those, since my knowledge of mathematics was rudimentary.

Finally, not knowing what else to do, I temporarily removed the "nineteen" that was common to all the numbers, but the sequence still seemed random. As I restored the first two digits, I wondered whether I had perhaps been looking in the wrong direction. I had struggled to make some mathematical sense of the eight numbers, but maybe what linked them was of a completely different nature.

Why would the author give me a mathematical puzzle, after all? Even if I were to find some pattern, what would be the purpose? Had the case been in its infancy, one could imagine that the author was toying with me by feeding me false leads, but events had moved on a long way from their starting point, so there was no time left for such a ploy. Regardless of what he was telling me with these numbers, it certainly was not just to toy with me.

The moment that the last "nineteen" was in place, it was as though a fog had lifted from my mind, one that had previously obscured my view. Focusing on the search for a mathematical pattern, I had not seen what was staring me in the face: the numbers were years.

In my excitement I rose from the armchair, then immediately settled back into it. I had no reason to be too pleased with myself. Even if it were to turn out that I was right about the years, that was only the first step. Next came an entire series of questions and I had no clue what the answers were: What did the eight years refer to? Why was it important to the author to reveal them to me in such a enigmatic way?—and perhaps the most important one: Why had he first put four additional digits and then removed them?

I covered my face with my hands and rubbed my forehead with the tips of my fingers, in an effort to recollect what I had only briefly glimpsed in the corridor on the third underground level, but the fog had still not cleared from there. The only vague impression that appeared was that the eight-digit numbers had the same fifth digit, but I couldn't make out what it was.

I pulled up the police database search and entered the eight years. There were six-and-a-half thousand hits, although not a single one contained all the years. There were none with seven, or even six of the years. I had expected that there would be many documents, since the search was rather ambiguous. There would certainly have been far fewer of them had I been able to provide any other information, but I had absolutely nothing.

Going through the six-and-a-half thousand hits in search of a clue would take hours, so it was out of the question at the moment. In any case, it wasn't necessary for only one person to do this. Undoubtedly an entire team of experts at the National Security Agency was at that very moment busy with this same task. I was sure they would immediately let me know if they dug anything up, in the spirit of true cooperation.

I switched off the computer and the monitor. Before returning the cell phone to my pocket I briefly illuminated the screen to see the time: five thirteen. It was as though this piece of information also reached my stomach; it started to rumble again. I left hastily, quickly locking up my office, then headed to the elevator. I smiled, thinking of how lucky I was, when the doors to the right-hand car opened without delay.

∽ 32 ∾

I pressed the button for the garage. The instant the two halves of the door came together, everything went dark. I sighed. So much for being lucky, or for the author ensuring good writing and not repeating himself. Well, that was his responsibility. Let's see what he had in store for me in this magic elevator. Hopefully he would not do what he did to Ms. Mirković—keep me inside for hours, regardless of the fact that it would seem quite brief to me and I wouldn't die of starvation. No excuse in the world would save me from the trouble I'd be in if I didn't make it to the reception that Vera wanted me to attend with her.

That's when it dawned on me that perhaps I would be spared the fate of the young lab technician. There were differences between what had befallen her and what was happening now. Everything had seemed normal to the girl: the lighting was on in the elevator the entire time; the darkness was there only for the camera that was concealed behind the mirror. Furthermore, she had felt the car move, but this time it was stationary. So, a different performance awaited me.

Just as I was starting to wonder what to do—whether to wait patiently for it to begin or perhaps take out my cell phone and cast some light around me—a familiar voice broke the silence, making me flinch.

"Here we are once again in the dark, Inspector Lukić," said the Grand Master.

It seemed to me that he was standing across from me, next to the elevator door, even though that was not possible. There was no way that he could have suddenly appeared in the cabin. The voice must be coming from a speaker, although I could swear that I was hearing him directly, just like in the attic of the City Cemeteries Administration Building.

Was that perhaps the explanation for his magical

disappearance from there? The Grand Master had not actually been in the attic at all, and it was the guard who had briefly held the flashlight pointed at me. That is why everything had transpired in sightlessness.

Once again I thought of turning on the phone screen and solving the mystery, but I gave up on it because there were more pressing matters. He had some reason for insisting on acting this way. He might have retreated if I'd tried to expose him; that could wait. Finding out why he had appeared now was more important than whether he was in the elevator or not.

"Feel free to turn on the light," I responded. "I have no objections."

"All in good time. It's better like this for the time being."

"You don't want me to see something?"

"Not you. There are other curious eyes."

"The camera behind the mirror? I'm blocking it. It's pointed at my back."

"It's not the only one. There are two more."

"Is that so?" I asked, honestly surprised.

"You mustn't allow yourself to be naive. The Agency will never tell you everything, even when it is actually cooperating with you."

"And what about sound? The darkness hasn't muted it. Don't you care that they can hear us?"

"They can't. We've taken care of that, of course."

"I assume you are aware that they are keeping a close eye on me. They know that I got into this elevator, but that it is still on the fifth floor. They will be here any moment to check what's going on."

"They won't. Don't underestimate us, Inspector Lukić. They think that you are still in the office."

"It seems that you have become more powerful than the National Security Agency."

"Now you're overestimating us. No one is more powerful than the Agency. We are just taking advantage of an opportunity. They are convinced that their main opponent is on the other side, so they're not paying much attention to us."

"They finally convinced me too, even though I had claimed for a long time that you were pulling the strings of everything that has happened today."

"I was the first one to tell you that it wasn't the case. You should have trusted me."

"If my memory serves me well, I don't have much reason to trust you. Wouldn't you tell me the same even if you were behind everything, but you wanted to keep it secret?"

"Nevertheless, I am glad that we are no longer your main suspects."

"You might not be the main suspects, but you are far from innocent. You are still making my life difficult. What is the purpose of this new ambush? What do you want from me?"

"You know very well what we want from you."

"*The Compendium of the Dead*? I don't have it. You know that. The three volumes that I received were taken by the National Security Agency. The fourth never appeared. I was just on my way home. I'm done for today. This entire case is not my concern anymore. If the volume that you are hoping for appears somewhere, you will have to discuss it with one of my colleagues on the next shift."

"Ah, if life were only that simple, that your worries stop when you punch out. Of course everything is still your concern. You are up to your neck in this case, whether you like it or not. And the fourth volume is just about to appear. Believe me when I say this, even if you won't believe the rest. I organized this meeting so that I could warn you one more time. Soon, when you find yourself holding *The Compendium of the Dead*, don't try to do anything with it on your own. You will cause immeasurable harm. Hand it over to us immediately—and finally you will be able to walk away from this case. Only then will it actually cease to be your concern."

I sighed. "It seems there's no point in telling you. . . ."

"I was afraid that you would be stubborn about this. All right, what can I do—you leave me no choice. Unfortunately, now I have to threaten you, even though the entire matter could have been settled without that. If you don't cooperate, we will have to relocate someone dear to you to *The Compendium of the Dead*. Someone very dear. Then you will scramble in panic to give us the books since you yourself will not be able to bring back that person from the *Compendium*. . . ."

I felt the blood rush to my face. I swiftly reached for the cell phone in my jacket pocket, but I wasn't fast enough. I had only got it half-way out when the lights went on and illuminated the car, which was empty except for me. The elevator departed for the garage at the same moment.

∽ 33 ∾

UNDER ANY OTHER CIRCUMSTANCES I would have used the descent, at least while I was alone, to try to find the National Security Agency's other two cameras. I would hardly be able to achieve anything in less than half a minute, and it was also possible that the Grand Master was not telling the truth, but I would not have been able to resist the temptation. Now, however, that was the least of my concerns. With fumbling thumbs I found Vera's number in my phonebook and called her.

It took great effort to keep a calm voice.

"How are you?" I asked, when she picked up.

"All right," she said, a little cautiously, as though surprised by my question. "And you?"

"I am too," I responded, then added with slight hesitation "More or less."

"You don't usually call me from your work phone."

"It was the one that was in my hand."

She was silent for a bit.

"Will you be home soon?"

"I'm on my way to the garage. I'll be at home shortly."

"Very well. . . ." she said, as though nothing better had come to mind.

Now it was my turn to fall briefly silent.

"You don't have any reason to go out until I get there?"

"No. . . ."

"Very well," I repeated in the same tone. "I'll see you then."

"See you. . . ."

The elevator doors opened onto the garage as I was returning the phone to my pocket. I reached my car in three steps. The moment I started the engine, my phone rang. I took it out again and glanced at the screen. I didn't recognize the number, but I knew who was calling.

"What happened, Inspector Lukić?" Agent Mirić asked.

"Wait a second." I took the phone headset out of the glove compartment, connected it to the telephone, dropped it on the adjacent seat and put the earphones in my ears. I had to drive fast, so I needed both hands; I could not be holding my cell phone in one. "I had a close encounter with the Grand Master," I said as I sped out of the garage.

"How close?"

"It seemed to me that he was with me in the elevator. In the dark."

This was followed by a pause while Mirić gave some-one brief instructions. I couldn't understand what he was saying.

"All right, we'll talk about it later. Is Miss Gavrilović in danger?"

"Maybe. . . ."

"We'll be there before you. I'll call you back soon."

"Thank you."

Barely three minutes had passed when he called me again.

"We have the house under surveillance. And we will be there shortly."

"Do you want to meet?"

"You'd better hurry over to Miss Gavrilović. We'll be close by."

"All right." I paused. "How is it that the Grand Master is better than you at dealing with the elevators at the Police Headquarters?"

"I don't know. We are investigating exactly what happened. So, you didn't see him?"

"I didn't. I could swear that he appeared in the elevator as soon as the lights went out, and disappeared a moment before the lights came back on, but as you know, he is a very skilled illusionist. By the way, he told me that you have two more cameras, in addition to the one behind the mirror, in the right-hand car."

"We do," he responded, after a slight hesitation.

"You didn't mention them to me."

"I would have if there had been any reason to. What did the Grand Master want this time?"

"The same as last time—*The Compendium of the Dead.*"

"Had he forgotten that we have the books?"

"No, he hadn't, of course. He isn't all that interested in the first three. He seems convinced that he will not have any difficulty getting a hold of them when he needs them. He cares about the fourth one."

"The fourth one is still nowhere to be found." He became silent for a moment. "Right?"

"Right, but he believes that it will turn up any time now. He threatened to kill someone very close to me. That way he would ensure that I handed the book over to him, because I would not be able to bring that person back from the dead using the *Compendium* on my own. And there is no one closer to me than Vera."

I could hear Mirić sigh over the phone.

"We'll move Miss Gavrilović somewhere immediately. She'll be safe, don't worry."

I thought of responding that I was still worried, that this event in the elevator was not the first time the Grand Master had outwitted the Agency, but I refrained. The young lead agent was doing everything he could. Even his significantly more experienced predecessor would not have had any greater success.

"Unfortunately, we will not be able to move her immediately. At seven o'clock we have to be at a reception that is very important to her. Can you provide a security detail for us?"

"Of course. Where is the reception being held?"

"I don't know. A car will be sent to pick us up at six thirty."

"Ask Miss Gavrilović."

"She doesn't know either."

"All right. Who is holding it?"

"She doesn't know that either. . . ."

Several moments passed in silence.

"The reception is very important to her, and she doesn't know anything about it?"

"It's a long story. We don't have time for it now. I'm almost there."

"Has it occurred to you that the Grand Master might be behind it all? That would be the easiest way for him to achieve his goal."

"It has," I lied. "We'll talk more about this. I'll speak to Vera."

"All right. We've freed a parking spot for you in front of the entrance. Do you see it?"

I was just entering Vera's street. "I see it. Thank you. By the way, have you made any sense of the numbers on the plates at the National Library?"

"Still nothing. We're working on it."

AFTER PARKING THE CAR I removed the earphones from my ears and the miniature jack from the cell phone, then placed the phone in my pocket. Even though my inclination towards neatness was quietly protesting, I did not waste any time returning the headset to the glove compartment. I briskly opened the car door and was already with my left foot on the ground, when a sudden thought stopped me mid-stride. I remained frozen in that position for several moments— neither out nor in.

I had a ghastly impression that there'd been a certain inconsistency in my short conversation with Agent Mirić. Something wasn't right, but I couldn't immediately put my finger on it. Pressured by haste I had almost given up, when it finally dawned on me. I jumped out of the car and ran to the building's entrance.

The first time we had met today, Mirić had told me that they hadn't let me out of their sight for the past eight months, since the "Grand Manuscript" case, and that this morning the alarm had been raised after I'd received the call from the City Cemeteries Administration. This meant among other things that they had been monitoring all the telephones that I use.

I had spoken on my private cell phone to Vera about the unusual offer that she had received, as well as what had happened later, including the mysterious reception that we were both invited to. Mirić would have been aware of that, but a moment ago it had seemed as though he didn't have a clue. There was no reason for him to pretend. He was aware that I knew that my phones were bugged; we had even mentioned it once.

How was this possible? The only explanation was that someone had foiled the Agency in monitoring my private cell phone. The question was not so much who could do it, but rather why. The Grand Master had demonstrated on several occasions that he was capable of performing incredible communications feats, but why would he resort to something so complex and risky?

Mirić himself had offered the answer. The Grand Master was actually the anonymous wealthy eccentric collector who had massively overpaid for the books and inventory from the Papyrus, and now he was holding the gala reception.

I had lied to Mirić, telling him that I had considered the possibility. It hadn't crossed my mind to connect what was happening today, apparently unrelatedly, with Vera and me. However, I should have put it together. Now, looking back, it didn't require any special insightfulness; actually, it was quite obvious.

Why did the Grand Master need the reception? That wasn't difficult to guess either. He had to have an audience for the miracle he was planning on performing—bringing people back from the dead using *The Compendium of the Dead*. And who better to resurrect than someone who had just died before the eyes of the large audience? Since one could not count on a natural death, however, it was necessary to resort to a violent one.

Someone needed to be murdered. Not just anyone, because the performance would sink into anticlimax—but someone whose death would touch everyone profoundly. Someone young, beautiful, innocent, who embodied the very fullness of life; an exceptional woman whose subsequent resurrection would be a unique triumph of the Grand Master.

Vera. . . .

I raced up the stairs, skipping two or three at a time.

The seven-story building that Vera lived in had an elevator, of course, but I used it only when I was with her. Even though she knew that I didn't take it when I was alone, she respectfully avoided teasing me about it, even though she otherwise enjoyed taunting me. Her conscience would not let her in this case. After what she had put me through with *The Grand Manuscript*, I was sure she felt at least partially to blame for my fear of elevators.

After returning eight months ago, Vera no longer shrunk from my study. She had seen the original in the other reality, so the copy no longer upset her. We could have lived in my place, we even spent two or three weeks in my apartment, but then she still proposed that we move to hers. She said that she felt more intimate there. Since it was all the same to me, and I also spent a lot less time at home than she did—I agreed.

For a while I didn't know what to do about my apartment. I could have sold it, but it didn't feel right. I was even less inclined to rent it out. In the end I didn't do anything. The apartment sat empty, and we went there from time to time for two or three days, for a change. Even though Vera didn't complain, I knew that she wasn't entirely pleased with this arrangement. She would occasionally tell me, in a teasing way, that I was keeping the apartment because I wasn't sure whether I wanted to stay with her.

On the third floor I realized that I couldn't have used the elevator even if I had wanted to. Two repairmen in dark blue overalls were busy working on it. I had almost run past them, when the one who was crouched down briefly looked up at me. I recognized him as one of the two young men who had carried out Inspector Vesić's body, and whom I had seen this morning, elegantly dressed, in the attic of the City Cemeteries Administration Building.

Panting, I stopped in front of the door to the middle apartment on the fourth floor, and started speedily going through my pants pockets, searching for the key. The door opened before I found it. Vera first looked at me speechlessly for several moments, then moved aside so that I could enter.

We stood across from each other in the hallway for a short while, then I hugged her tightly. We stayed like that for some time. Vera was the first to break the silence.

"Have you eaten anything since this morning?"

I looked at her confusedly, as though she were asking me something utterly bizarre. Finally I shook my head.

"Come." She nodded towards the dining room.

"No, stop. I have to tell you. . . ."

"You can tell me while you're eating."

And so I ate and talked. I condensed nearly nine hours of the long day into twenty-five minutes. I didn't leave anything out. Not even the suspicion about what role she was to play in the Grand Master's performance. It was only after Vera had cleared the table that I realized that I had not noticed what I had been eating.

～ 35 ～

I STAYED SEATED IN the dining room while Vera was in the kitchen. I was suddenly overcome by fatigue. I had not had a break since morning. The work of a police inspector is dynamic and tense, but events this packed together exist only in novels. That is why even the digest could not be any shorter.

Talking between bites exhausted me additionally. Also, after the large meal, it was as though all the blood from my head had rushed to my stomach, and I was overcome by sluggishness, drowsiness. It seemed very tempting just to sit like this, staring in front of me and listening to the muffled noises from the kitchen. I was, however, aware that this idyll could not last. The extraordinary day was most definitely not over. The main excitement was yet to come.

Vera returned carrying two steaming cups of coffee. She placed them on the table and sat down next to me. She still had not said anything about all that she had heard. She had gone to the kitchen not so much to do the dishes and make coffee, as to gather her thoughts. She still appeared contemplative.

"I should have let you know earlier," I said, "but for a long time I wasn't sure what was actually going on. Anyway, cell phones are not reliable. . . ."

"I should have realized it myself. My entire life I've ridiculed people willing to believe even the most incredible nonsense if it suits them, and now that is exactly how I have behaved. I mean really—a 'wealthy eccentric collector'. . . ."

"You can't blame yourself. Anyone would have done the same. Nothing seemed suspicious to me either."

The shadow of a smile passed across her face. I thought that she might make a remark about my insightfulness—that topic never ceased to entertain her—but she immediately turned serious again.

"Perhaps you can learn something more from the Samardžić Law Offices, the broker. They wouldn't tell me anything about the buyer, but I guess they would have to share it with the police."

"If not with the police, then certainly with the National Security Agency. It is unlikely, however, that they know very much. I'm sure that the Grand Master was careful. He had no reason to handle it personally. One of his people took care of that job—anonymously and discreetly. In any case, all that isn't important any more."

"But could you at least dig up where the reception is being held? It was important to the attorneys that I commit to both of us attending, as though they were personally interested in it. Perhaps they do know something."

"There's no more time. And there's no need. We'll learn about the location of the reception from the chauffeur who comes to pick us up. He will have to know where to take us."

Vera didn't reply. The seriousness on her face seemed to change to concern. I quickly tried to calm her.

"Don't worry. I'm with you now. I won't leave you even for a moment until all this is over. The people from the Agency are also here, all around us. You're completely safe."

She continued to watch me in silence, her expression unchanged.

"The Grand Master can't touch you. First of all, we don't have to go to that reception at all. Also, he won't try anything until he has all the parts of *The Compendium of the Dead*, and the last one has still not shown up. I would know if it had. The first three books were sent to me. There is no reason for the fourth one not to be."

She looked at me for several more seconds, then she said something completely unexpected.

"Why don't you take a bath? It would do you good, and you need to change if we end up going to the reception."

I looked at her questioningly.

"Come on. I'll run you a bath."

I followed her into the bathroom without asking any questions. We didn't have a bathtub, only a shower.

She closed the door after us, then turned on the hot water in the shower. The room started to fill with steam.

"I saw this in a movie once," she said softly, with a bashful smile, as though justifying her action. I had to strain my ears to understand her over the running water. "Is it possible that the Grand Master is listening in on us in the apartment?"

"I don't know. I don't believe so, but it isn't entirely impossible. Why?"

"I have something to tell you that definitely is not for his ears."

She didn't tell me immediately. The mist around us was getting thicker. Vera seemed to fade away into it, even though she was standing only one step from me.

"The fourth volume has appeared," came a whisper from the mist.

"Where? When?" I responded with questions, also softly.

"Here. Less than an hour ago."

"Here?"

"Not in our apartment but in the basement. The small apartment of our neighbor, Mr. Ljuštanović, the retired speleologist, whose wife died about fifteen years ago, and he still visits her grave every day. Remember him?"

"Yes. The old man who raves about life underground. His windows are full of yellow flowers."

"That's right. He was leaving for his afternoon walk, and found an envelope with your name on his door-mat. He brought it up immediately."

"Where did you put it?"

"On the shelf with the books from the weirdoes. I was convinced that was what it was. That's why I didn't even call you. It even crossed my mind that the old man had made up that he had found the envelope in front of his door. He needed an excuse to send you something. He does seem like a patient."

"It's good that you didn't call me. The book would already be in the hands of the Grand Master." At the last moment I stopped myself from adding: "And who knows what would have happened to you."

"Should I bring you the envelope together with your change of clothes? I can do it discreetly. They won't notice anything if there are cameras."

I turned towards the shower and turned off the water.

"There aren't any microphones or cameras. If there were, they would have immediately understood what Mr. Ljuštanović had brought and they would have been here instantly. We're safe in the apartment."

I left the bathroom and entered the small room that

Vera had given me to use as a study, even though I hadn't asked her. I kept some of my books there. She had added the rest—a desk and everything else that a writer might need. She had never proposed anything to that effect. The things were there in case the need ever arose.

Vera had placed the envelope horizontally on top of the books that filled one section of the shelf. I picked it up and examined it from both sides. It did not differ in any way from the previous three. I opened it, took out the white volume and leafed through it quickly. It was identical to the others. I handed it to Vera, who had come into the room with me.

"This is what everything is revolving around this time. The new dark object of desire of the Grand Master and his band."

Vera scrutinized the book for several minutes. She felt the strange paper, smelled it, at one moment it even looked as though she might lick it, but she just held it close to her lips. Just as I had done that morning, she raised a page to the light coming through the window. She didn't say anything. When she had finished, she didn't know what to do with the volume for a moment, but finally returned it to me. I too had second thoughts before laying it down on the desk.

"Truly an unusual book," she said finally. "What will you do with it?"

I shrugged my shoulders. "I don't know. I should hand it over to the people from the Agency, but the Grand Master has hinted that he could get his hands on the volumes that are in their safe. Perhaps it is best if I leave it here for now." I pointed to the shelf from which I had taken the envelope. "It is in good company there. Also, it is better that no one finds out that it has appeared. As long as that remains the case, the Grand Master will not harm you."

Vera was silent for several moments, then she shook her head.

"Something doesn't add up, Dejan. If my murder and resurrection are supposed to be the highlight of the Grand Master's performance, why would he announce it to you during your conversation in the elevator? He not only gave away his main surprise, but also warned us."

"He had to threaten me with something in order to ensure that I would give him the fourth volume, and he knows that that is where I am most vulnerable."

"He didn't have to. If he had already expected to get a hold of the volumes from the Agency's safe, why didn't he just let you give it to the agents, and then simply take all four?"

I tried to come up with an answer quickly, but to no avail.

"I don't know."

"That's not all. The reception is scheduled for seven o'clock in the evening. How could the Grand Master be certain that he would have all the volumes in time? Look, the fourth one is still not in his hands, and there isn't much time left until seven."

I looked at her for a short while without speaking.

"What are you trying to say?"

"I mean that there is to be no performance by the Grand Master. He only wants the fourth volume. If he gets it, he has no reason to harm me."

"Are you proposing that we hand it over to him?" I asked in disbelief.

"I propose that you give it to the Agency. Let them deal with the Grand Master."

Now I shook my head.

"I can't take that risk. The safest thing is for the book to remain here. Even if it is true that there is to be no performance by the Grand Master, he could still hurt you in order to get back at me. He said that he sees me as his main adversary. I assume he would not take it lightly if he were to suffer a third defeat, following the Last Book and the Grand Manuscript."

Vera smiled at me.

"There is no risk, Dejan. The Grand Master could not touch me even if he wanted to. I have a powerful protector."

I smiled back.

"I'm not that powerful. . . ."

"I don't mean you, but the author."

I blinked. "The author?"

"Yes. The author would never allow anything to happen to me."

"Really? How do you know?"

"I know. Trust me. I'll explain it on another occasion. There's no time to discuss that now. It's past six o'clock. Go back to the bathroom; I'll bring your clothes. I too have to get ready. Don't forget, this isn't just an ordinary reception."

"Are you sure you want us to go?"

"Pass up something like that?"

"But who is holding the reception, if it isn't the Grand Master?"

"We'll learn soon enough. Hurry up."

$\backsim$ 36 $\backsim$

I HURRIED, BUT NOT so much that I couldn't stop at the dining room table and drink the cup of coffee in several large gulps. It was already lukewarm, but it felt very good. I could almost feel it dispel the last traces of drowsiness.

Before entering the bathroom I left the things that I would not need that evening on the dresser: my private cell phone, key ring and plastic gloves. I also pulled out of my pockets my work phone, badge and wallet, but I took them with me, to put in the other suit. Of course, I would be carrying my gun in a shoulder holster.

In front of the bathroom door I passed by Vera, who had already brought me a change of clothes. She smiled at me devilishly, then ran into the bedroom to get ready. I wasn't exactly happy about her joyfulness. What was about to happen was not to be taken lightly. It now seemed to me that this was exactly how I had acted when I agreed that we should go to the reception. I had caved in to her assertion, but what if both she and I had missed something? What if we were thoughtlessly walking into a trap that the Grand Master had set for us?

I undressed and was already in the shower when my cell phone rang. I got out and took the phone from the shelf beneath the mirror, where I had placed it with the other things.

"Agent Mirić," I said, "I was just about to call you. We have decided to attend the reception. As I have told you, a car is picking us up at six thirty. I still don't know where they are taking us. Question the chauffeur. In any case, we are counting on your security detail."

"Of course. I have some news. We have discovered the meaning of the numbers in the pictures that you took at the National Library."

"What is it?" I asked anxiously, then quickly added "You can also tell me when we meet in a short while, if you think that it isn't safe now."

"It's safe. We're using a double secure line."

"All right. I'm listening."

"They are the birth years of the eight victims in the two cases of crossing realities; six from the first and two from the second."

The line was mute for several moments.

"Inspector Lukić?"

"I'm here. I was just thinking."

"Do you have any idea why those years were placed above the doors on the third underground level?"

This was the right moment for me to reveal what I had been keeping from them. They didn't deserve that I should act that way. They hadn't betrayed our cooperation even once. On the contrary, it was I who had done so. However, I didn't share his trust in the double secure line. One should never underestimate the Grand Master. For that reason I decided to keep to myself the appearance of the fourth volume of *The Compendium of the Dead*. He would get it as soon as we went downstairs, and I would also tell him about the numbers missing from the pictures.

"I have to think about it. We'll talk soon."

"All right."

I put down the phone and returned to the shower. I set the water temperature, then stood beneath the spray. The hot swarm of needlelike droplets stung the top of my head and my shoulders. The water first washed away only the physical deposits of the difficult day. Then it began to remove the accumulated tension and fatigue, and finally it started to scatter the wisps of fog that had settled around in my mind.

In the clarity that was gradually expanding I tried to revive the memory of what I had only glimpsed in the underground corridor at the National Library, and which had later mysteriously disappeared from the photos. I could now clearly see the first four digits, but those following them were still a blur.

I pressed the tips of my fingers against my temples, squeezed my eyes shut and bowed my head, but nothing helped. The second four digits still appeared as though through a dense condensation on the glass. Obsessed by my frustration, I crouched down. I had somehow to see past that murkiness but I didn't know how.

I was already eager to get up and exit the shower— Vera must have been annoyed by my delay—when it occurred to me that I might know a way of revealing what was hidden. If hot water could not dispel the cloudiness, perhaps cold water could.

Unlike Vera, who loved showering under cold water, I was horrified by the notion. I couldn't hesitate for a moment, otherwise I would surely change my mind. I rose quickly, grabbed the tap and moved it in the opposite direction. It took great will not to bounce to the opposite corner of the shower, out of the range of the icy stream.

I endured about ten seconds in it, although it seemed a lot longer to me. I was frozen stiff. I could barely move my hand to switch off the water. I remained shivering for a while, waiting for the heat that filled the bathroom to engulf me again.

And then it happened. As I was thawing out, the condensation on the glass dissipated and beneath it the outlines of the numbers emerged. Staring at the steam that was retreating to the shower cubicle, I clearly saw in my memory what had been beyond my reach only a moment ago.

The cold water was not the only thing responsible for this apparition. Something Agent Mirić had just said had contributed equally. "Six from the first and two from the second." The digits that had disappeared from the photos formed only two numbers: 2013 appeared six times, and 2014 appeared twice.

The years of the deaths of the eight victims from the cases of crossing realities.

Of course, I should have been pleased with myself, but the feeling of frustration came over me again. I should have recognized this back there, in the corridor. I had already seen one of the eight numbers; albeit it had a dash in the middle, but nonetheless. How many times had I stood in front of Olga's grave and looked at the numbers carved beneath her name on the tombstone: "1980-2013"?

There was a knock on the door. "Are you finished?" Vera asked impatiently.

"I'll be right out," I responded, then got out of the shower and grabbed a towel. I was only half done wiping myself when something occurred to me. I flung the towel over my shoulder and took the cell phone from the shelf. My fingers danced across the small keypad. I sent Mirić the two photos I had taken the last time I was at the City Cemeteries Administration. With them I included the text: *"Call Mrs. Leleković; have her find out from which years are the two books that are missing from the shelf. Urgently."*

As I hastily dressed, my thoughts fervently and un-successfully spun around the question why the years of the deaths of the eight victims in the "Last Book" and the "Grand Manuscript" cases would be erased from the photos taken in the National Library. What was the meaning of that move? What was the author trying to tell me?

Mirić's text message arrived as I was tying my necktie. *"2013 and 2014. Your limo is here."*

I had received confirmation of what I had suspected, but I still wasn't satisfied. I had to ask the administrator immediately. It could not have been irrelevant which books Trpimirović had taken.

"We'll be down in a few minutes," I answered Mirić.

Vera looked at me grumpily when I came out of the bathroom. "Even I would not have taken that long."

"You only get ready in the bathroom, I also do work there." I looked her over. She was wearing a dark blue tweed suit and a matching lighter blouse. "So, that's what you've chosen."

"You don't like it?"

"On the contrary. It looks very good on you. You wore something similar when we first met, didn't you?"

"You remember? I'm impressed."

"Perhaps I'm not famous for my insightfulness, but I have an excellent memory."

"Speaking of insightfulness. . . ."

"We'll discuss that later," I interrupted. "I've re-ceived word that the limo is here. I'll just go get the white book, and we can be on our way."

Vera nodded, then went to the coat rack in the hallway to put on her coat, and I went to the study. I stopped at the door, however, and stared at the desk in confusion. The fourth volume of *The Compendium of the Dead* was not where I had left it.

◠ 37 ◠

"DID YOU TAKE THE book?" I asked Vera as I turned towards the hallway. I instantly realized that the question was redundant. Had she taken it she would have immediately told me so when I said I was going to fetch it.

"I didn't," she responded. She walked over to me as she put on her coat and looked first at the desk, then at me. "Where is it?"

"Did you hear any noise while I was in the bathroom? Anything at all?"

She shook her head. "Nothing, except the muffled sound of water."

I stepped into the study and checked the windows. They were all closed. I did the same in the other rooms. Not a single one was open. I finally went to the apartment door and saw for myself that it was locked, with the key in the lock. Vera followed my every step.

"How could it have disappeared?" she asked.

"There are only two possibilities: the Grand Master or the author."

"How could the Grand Master enter a closed apartment without making a sound, take the book and leave, with everything teeming with people from the Agency? He is exceptionally skillful, but he's not a wizard. And how would he even know that the fourth volume was here? You said yourself that there was no surveillance."

I shrugged. "I have no idea. I know only that he should never be dismissed. I have seen that for myself many times."

"Be that as it may, there's nothing we can do about the book's disappearance now, regardless of which of them has it. In any case, we don't even need it. On the contrary, life will be simpler without it. Let someone who cares deal with it. Let's go."

"Perhaps it would better if we didn't go to that reception. . . ."

"Don't be afraid. I told you that the author is watching over us. Nothing will happen to us."

I would have continued to discourage her had she not said "Don't be afraid." This way I had no choice—was I supposed to seem like a coward? I too put on my coat, touched my gun holster under my shoulder, unlocked the door and peered outside.

The supposed elevator repairs had moved to our floor in the meantime. The lights in the corridor were off, and the only illumination came from the open elevator car, where two men in dark-blue overalls were busy. When one got up and started walking towards me, I thought it was the one I had recognized on the third floor, but it turned out to be Mirić. He had earpieces in both ears.

I opened the door, stepped into the corridor, and then signaled Vera to join me. She slipped out, turned around and quickly locked the door.

"Agent Mirić," I presented the false repairman to her. She nodded. "I know."

I looked at her questioningly.

"He appears in my novel, remember?" she said with a smile.

Mirić also lightly bowed and smiled, and then took a small flashlight out from one of his many pockets and pointed the thin beam towards the stairwell.

He and I went in front, Vera was in the middle, and the rear was taken by the other agent, who had also stepped out of the car in the meantime. Mirić chose the stairs instead of the elevator, obviously on account of what had happened earlier at the Police Headquarters.

Despite the poor visibility, we descended at a fast pace, so I started to speak quickly and softly. I wouldn't get a better opportunity to share the new information with Mirić, without the fear that someone might overhear us. Luckily I didn't have to explain much to him.

"The fourth volume was brought to Vera by the neighbor living in the basement. He found it on his doormat this afternoon. The book is the same as the others. I was going to give it to you, but it disappeared from my desk while we were getting ready. Did you notice anything unusual?"

"Nothing. The first three volumes have also disappeared from our safe. I was notified a little while ago."

"That could not be the Grand Master. Nevertheless, we should be cautious. He's still in the game."

"I agree."

Another figure emerged silently from the darkness on the third floor and joined us at the rear of our column.

"About the numbers on the plates: there are only four digits recorded on the photos, but I saw eight on each one down there. Now I know what the missing four digits represent—the years of death of the eight victims in the two cases of crossing realities."

"Those two that Administrator Leleković mentioned—2013 and 2014?"

"Exactly."

"Why were they removed?"

"I don't know."

On the second floor the column was joined by another member.

"The limousine and chauffeur were hired; an anonymous client. The chauffeur doesn't know where he is supposed to take you. He will get instructions en route, via GPS. He will not receive them if anyone other than the two of you gets in."

"You've checked the car?"

"We have. Everything seems clean."

"Are you ready to tail it?"

"Absolutely. Reinforcements are here. We won't lose sight of you."

In the darkness of the ground floor there were four more agents waiting for us. They were joined by two of the three from our group, and all went out in front of the door and lined the path to the street. Raising his hand, Mirić stopped me. He himself exited, while holding the fingers of his left hand to his ear and speaking softly. He looked left, right, and up. Then he gave us the signal to move.

I turned around and smiled at Vera, then took her by the hand and led her out. I couldn't see her face very well in the shadows. I positioned myself to shield her with my body as much as possible. The six agents closed ranks, and Mirić went in front of us. He quickly opened the large white rear door of the limo and stepped aside. I pushed Vera inside, then slipped in after her. The door closed instantly.

The limo set off at the same moment. It was only then that I became aware of its size. It must have been at least as long as two regular cars. We sat in the rear white leather seat and were almost two meters from the rear-facing front seat. Above the backrest was a tinted glass partition, so we couldn't see the driver. The windows around us were also tinted. Through them we could only catch glimpses of bright lights as we passed by. No sound from the outside world could be heard.

"What did I tell you?" said Vera, leaning back into the wide soft seat. "A real limo, like in the movies."

"There are several of them in the city. They are mostly rented by the *nouveau riche* to strut around in when they have something to celebrate."

"I'm sure there are also police chiefs among them."

"I wouldn't know, I'm just an ordinary inspector." I paused for a moment. "I see that you are taking everything in a spirit of fun."

"It's always more pleasant that way. Tomorrow it will be especially fun when I once again leave the house I live in—and there isn't half the National Security Agency outside protecting me."

"They may have saved your life. And mine."

"I told you not to be afraid. We are under better protection than anything the Agency can offer."

I leaned over to her ear and whispered: "Let's stick to neutral topics. We don't know who might be listening."

She scowled at me.

"Neutral? All right, here's one. At the moment we are in no hurry, so we can talk about it. Have you figured out what it is that I can finally do? What it is that I have always fantasized about? You have very little time left. The deadline expires at seven, as you are well aware. You have to give me an answer before we leave this limousine."

I sighed. "You know what my day has been like. . . ."

"Will a slightly stressful day thwart your famous insightfulness?"

"Slightly stressful?"

"Don't use the day as an excuse. Even on the most stressful of days you have to know the soul of the woman you are living with."

"Insightfulness is not enough for that. One needs to be clairvoyant. How about you help me a little?"

"The famous Inspector Lukić needs help? He can't solve a simple problem on his own? Well, all right, what can we do? It is an art, of course."

"Is it, now?"

"Why are you surprised?"

"I'm not surprised, I just had no idea."

"You would have had some idea if you paid more attention to what I said, and especially if you paid attention to what I didn't say."

"Now you expect me to be telepathic as well?"

"Why not? That would be useful for your job too. So?"

"You want to continue writing?"

"God forbid. How did you come up with that?"

"Well, you tried to be a writer. . . ."

"That one time was quite enough. In any case, you see the trouble prose creates. Next."

"Music? You want to write music?"

"I would like to, but unfortunately I have no real talent for music."

"What's left? Sculpting? No, you're not . . . muscular enough."

"You've gone through every possibility except the right one. You've really disappointed me."

"Painting?" I asked in amazement.

"Painting, of course."

"How could I have guessed that? You've never given me any hint."

"I didn't have to. All it would take is to connect two details that you know about me."

"Details?"

"Yes. Before I couldn't be a painter because I didn't see colors. Now I see them."

I gazed at Vera, not knowing what to say. The amusing conversation had suddenly become serious. She stared back at me, expecting me to say something.

What got me out of the predicament was the fact that the limo suddenly slowed down, then stopped. The barely noticeable vibration stopped, as the driver turned off the engine. I turned towards the door, expecting, for some reason, that someone would open it. When that did not happen after about fifteen seconds, I carefully opened it a little and peered outside.

We were on a well-lit street. Through the narrow opening I saw the window of a pharmacy. It seemed familiar but I couldn't remember where I had seen it. The passersby turned curiously to see the long white limousine. I waited a little longer, then slowly opened the door all the way and stepped outside, signaling Vera to wait.

What I saw was not supposed to be there. I stared for a while in disbelief at the sight in front of me, as though it had magically emerged from the past, then I hurried to offer Vera my hand so that she might join me. To her this would be an even greater surprise.

∽ 38 ∾

I CLOSED THE DOOR after Vera. The limo immediately drove off, freeing up at least two parking spaces. When it had moved away down the street, pedestrians no longer had any reason to take notice of the couple that had come out of it, who now remained standing by the curb, gazing at the nearby window.

I looked around, hoping to spot the agents who were tailing us, but there was no sign of them. That didn't concern me. Actually, it would have been unusual if I had noticed them. I thought of getting in touch with Agent Mirić, but he would have already called me if something was wrong.

A cosmetics store was supposed to be in front of us. It had been there several days earlier when I had had passed by, going about my business. There had been no indication that it was closing. On the contrary, inside it had been teeming with customers, as usual. I remembered then what had crossed my mind the first time that I saw the shop: we live in an era when people care much more about quick body beautification than the slow beautification of the soul.

Now, however, everything was different.

The metal and glass, the kitsch glamour, were gone, and the previous antique nobility reigned once again. Instead of the products of the famous cosmetics chain, the shop was full of books, as it has been up until two years earlier. Above the shop window the glittering Fragrance neon sign had given way to discreet and elegant lettering reading Papyrus.

It seemed, however, that there was a price that had to be paid for restoring the bookshop. As far as I could see through the window and the door—there was no one inside.

I didn't rush Vera. For a while she just stared at the Papyrus, without saying a word. The barely perceptible quiver in the corner of her lips gave away how excited she was. She finally turned towards me and looked at me inquisitively. I shrugged, not knowing how to respond to her tacit questions.

Then I led her to the entrance. I paused with my hand on the doorknob before turning it. We were greeted by the sound of ringing bells. After stepping inside, we stayed next to the door, hesitating to go in any deeper, as though we might break the spell of the resurrection of the Papyrus.

Our eyes passed over the multitude of colorful volumes on the shelves, the armchairs lined with worn-out dark-green plush, the blossoming potted plants, the neatly arranged ornaments on the mantelpiece above the small lit fireplace, the cash register counter.

"Perfect," Vera said first, quietly. "Everything is perfect. . . ."

She went up to the shelf to the left of the shop window. She raised her hand and for a moment held it in front of the books, then laid her fingertips on the spines. She walked along the wall, running her fingers across the packed volumes, as though she needed to touch them to be absolutely certain that they were real. Having circled most of the room, she also touched the mantelpiece and the backs of all four armchairs the same way. Finally she approached the counter and pressed something. The cash register drawer opened with a rasping sound. Smiling, she pushed it back, then nodded for me to join her.

I stopped in front of the cash register and looked around once more.

"As far as I can remember, it looks the same, down to the smallest detail."

"Not only looks, but is. This is the old Papyrus, not a reconstruction. The books are the same, the furniture, the things, details, the whole lot. Even the place is the same."

"The place was certainly very expensive. The owners of the Fragrance chain had no reason to sell the shop. Their business was booming. They must have been made an offer that they could not refuse."

"It's easy for the author to make such offers in his novel. Money is not a issue there; he can have as much of it as he wants."

"Lucky him. But why do you think he brought the Papyrus back to life?"

"Who knows? Perhaps for some sentimental reason he had the desire to hold the reception right here. If you have more money than you know what to do with, you are in a position to indulge your whims."

I shook my head. "That would be very *nouveau riche*, and the author is not like that. We both know him; what's more, such whims would put the novel in jeopardy. No, it must be something else, something deeper."

"Deeper?"

"What will happen to the Papyrus after the reception is over?"

Vera shrugged her shoulders. "Fragrance will replace it again. Perhaps the author didn't buy the shop but only rented it short-term."

"If it were so, he would not have gone to the trouble of reviving the old Papyrus in every little detail."

"Then he will keep it closed, until a new reception or some similar occasion. Why not? He can afford to."

"That too would be a *nouveau riche* whim."

Vera hesitated for a brief moment before responding. "As far as I can see, there is only one option remaining—he is planning to reopen the bookstore."

I nodded. "That is the only thing that makes sense. The old Papyrus is not back only temporarily; it's here to stay."

Vera watched me in silence for several moments.

"Yet this is not the old Papyrus in every way. It can never again be that. The bookstore is not only the inventory and the place, but also the people who run it. And they are no more. . . ."

"One of the two women who founded and ran the Papyrus is still here. . . ."

"Didn't I just tell you that I am planning to focus on painting?"

"One thing does not exclude the other. You can both run the bookstore and paint."

"I don't want to run the bookstore; you are well aware of that."

Now it was I who was silent for a moment.

"I'd say that the author is counting on getting you to change your mind. He wouldn't go to all this trouble if he wasn't sure. He is aware that without you there is no bringing back the Papyrus, and he obviously really cares about that."

"How could he get me to change my mind?"

"With a new offer that you won't be able to refuse."

Vera's voice quivered. "If you mean money. . . ."

"Of course I don't mean money," I interrupted her, jumping in to eliminate the misunderstanding.

"Then what?"

"I have no clue. How can I know what is in an author's head? I'm just a piteous uninsightful police inspector."

I pulled my lips into a contrite smile, which in turn made her smile.

"Take off your coat," she said as she started removing her own. "They've really turned up the heat."

I stood briefly, unsure where to put it away. Vera got me out of the predicament.

"Give it to me; I'll put them over there."

She turned around and went towards the back room behind the counter, but it was locked.

"That's odd," she said. "We always kept the back room unlocked; I don't even know where the key is." She came back to the register and placed the two coats on the counter, then looked at her delicate wristwatch. "Seven thirteen. Were only the two of us invited to the reception? Not only are there no other guests, but the host is also missing."

I looked towards the entrance. "Someone is bound to turn up. Let me take advantage of the fact that we are still alone to ask you something. I didn't have a chance in that crowd before we came here. You spent almost a year and a half with the author. Have you ever seen his handwriting?"

Vera thought for a second. "I have. He showed me his notepad where he had written one of his short novels in pencil. Why?"

"Would you be able to recognize it if you saw it again?"

"I think so. It's rather specific—the letters are small, square, almost printed."

"It's not the handwriting on the envelope that the neighbor Ljuštanović brought you?"

"No, it's not," Vera answered unwaveringly. "That was large, round; it doesn't at all look like the author's. Why?" she repeated her question.

"I'm trying to solve one of the many riddles that I've been given in the new novel. If it isn't the author's handwriting on the four envelopes, then whose is it?"

"Does it really matter? The author knew that I would recognize his handwriting, so he asked someone to write the inscription on the envelopes. It doesn't make any difference who it is."

"There was no reason to involve another person. The text could have been printed."

"Why then was it written by hand?"

I was silent for a few moments, then spoke softly, as though saying something in confidence. "Because that would be an opportunity for the novel's real author to leave his signature."

Vera squinted. "Real author?"

"Yes. We all assume that this is the author's new novel, but it doesn't necessarily have to be so. Perhaps the author is a mentor again, as he was to you in the previous case, while someone else is writing the novel."

"Who?"

I shook my head. "I don't know."

"Even the Agency can't determine whose handwriting it is?"

"They are still trying."

"Could all this be just a trick by the author; using the unidentified handwriting on the envelopes to try to get you to believe that he is a mentor, while in fact he is writing the novel?"

"That's also a possibility, but there are other indications that it is a different author."

"For example?"

"This novel is missing something that the author stuck to in the previous two. For example, my dreams, without which I could not find the answers."

"That is only because everything is happening in the course of one day." Vera smiled. "One cannot expect a police inspector to sleep on the job, even if it helped him solve cases."

"It wasn't necessary for everything to happen in one day. The author chose so himself. Also, the teashop is also gone. It has a pivotal place both in *The Last Book* and *The Grand Manuscript*. In *The Compendium of the Dead* I haven't even smelled tea."

"So, that is the title of the new novel—*The Compendium of the Dead*?"

"I guess. What would be more fitting? However, the

most important is the third thing—there are no bodies."

"You don't know that. Three people have disappeared
without a trace. It could turn out that they are dead.
Then there will be more victims than in my novel."

"I doubt it. We have been given a hint as to what will
happen to the missing persons. Among other things,
that is the purpose of the episode with the lab technician. We can expect their miraculous return."

"The novel still isn't finished. Someone might be
killed at the reception."

"If this turns out to be a reception only for the two
of us—that threat is excluded. You are convinced that
you enjoy the author's protection, and I think that I can
hope for it too. However, even if the Papyrus fills with
people, no one will be killed."

"You can't be certain of that."

"I can. The purpose of this work is to achieve exactly what you had aimed for—to show that a detective
novel is in fact possible without murder victims. I was
mistaken when I claimed that it was impossible."

"If no one will be killed at the reception, then what
will happen at it? This is supposed to be novel's finale.
What dénouement awaits us? What is there to resolve?
The return of three missing persons, even if it is miraculous, is hardly a grand finale."

I nodded. "That's a very good question. Unfortunately I don't have an answer. I have only a certain
premonition that the dénouement has been announced
in the events of today, but any kind of clearer picture
eludes me."

"What do you mean?"

"First of all, ever since it became evident that realities have crossed again, I have not been able shake
the feeling that whoever is pulling the strings from
the other reality is doing so in such a way as to make
my life difficult. He is confronting me with unsolvable

riddles, clouding everything around me as soon as it seems to me that I have understood something, and giving me false leads. I am constantly being led astray. It is as though he is angry with me and is taking revenge, although benevolently. At the same time it is as though he is indicating to me something very significant, which he must not reveal prematurely; something that he is keeping for the very end of the book."

"I don't understand you."

"I don't understand very well either. Here's an example. Death appears as a leitmotif in all of today's episodes. In the case of Mr. Trpimirović, the archivist, it is most apparent—actually there is nothing but death around him. Mrs. Ognjanović and Miss Šuvaković were very excited about *The Book of Resurrection*. The old poet, Vidojević is doing penance for the collection *Small Poems of Death*. Finally, our neighbor, Ljuštanović, has been visiting the cemetery every day for the past decade and a half."

"Those are all more or less serious forms of necrophilia, if you ask me."

"Perhaps it's not only that. There are other leitmotifs. All four books appeared in underground spaces: the Archive of the City Cemeteries Administration Building, the National Library Department of Old and Rare Books, the poet's cellar, and in front of our neighbor's basement apartment. Yellow flowers are another commonality of those places. There are some in the police lab as well, which is also underground." I paused a little. "Also, as I mentioned earlier, there is the imitation of the behaviors of patients from the Papyrus: someone first switched books around on the shelves, then placed a valuable volume in the library, and lastly—the copious purchases of copies of the same work."

"So what is the meaning of it all?"

"I don't know. I just have the feeling that it cannot be meaningless. It isn't just random. Finally, the four missing persons are connected to the underground, which weighs heavily on them in different ways. They all want to free themselves from it. The poet's wife is no exception. She lives in an apartment that looks like it doesn't have any windows."

"That's natural. No one feels pleasant underground."

"No, of course not, but there is something more here; this aspiration—like everything else—seems to have a certain symbolic meaning. However, I am missing the key to that symbolism. Perhaps I might find it if I could figure out who the author of the new novel is. It seems to me that everything would become simpler."

Vera watched me expressionlessly for several instants, then smiled.

"Perhaps it isn't that difficult to find out who the author is this time. It wasn't difficult even when the writer was my mentor. All it took was asking the right question."

"What question?"

"Who is absent from our reality? Who isn't here, and is connected to the events?"

At that very moment the bells above the entrance rang sharply.

∽ 39 ∽

WRAPPED UP IN OUR conversation, we were both startled by the unexpected noise and turned around swiftly. It took me a moment to recognize the man who had entered; I had only ever seen him in a white lab coat. Dr. Dimitrijević, the pathologist, looked distinguished in his three-piece gray suit, with a wide tie of the same shade. We hadn't seen each other since the "Last Book" case.

He came up to us and bowed to Vera. "Good evening, Miss Gavrilović. I am very honored by your invitation to the reopening of the Papyrus." He turned to me, missing her confused look. "Inspector Lukić, it's nice to meet you on a pleasurable occasion at last."

"We are glad that you were able to come, Dr. Dimitrijević," I rushed to preempt Vera, who had already opened her mouth to express her bewilderment.

"How could I miss it? When you are in my line of work, you only get invited to somber events. This is truly a welcome change. I only hope that I won't bring you any bad luck. They say that Thanatos follows me everywhere." He smiled awkwardly, as though apologizing. His propensity for dark humor had obviously not abandoned him.

"Don't worry, Doctor. Thanatos will not dare even look at the Papyrus. We're protected by Eros."

"There's another reason I'm glad to be here. To my great disgrace, I can't remember the last time I stopped by a bookstore. I would like to take the opportunity to have a look at the books, while it still isn't crowded."

"Please do."

Without waiting for Dr. Dimitrijević to move away enough, Vera muttered through clenched lips: "Only the reception was mentioned. There was no suggestion of reopening the Papyrus."

"That's how it is when you deal with lawyers. Legally speaking, they didn't deceive you. This is obviously the reception for the reopening of the Papyrus. You should have gotten the details before agreeing to come."

"And what should I do now? The Doctor is convinced that I'm behind the invitation. Others will surely think the same."

"Let them think it."

"What do you mean—let them think it?" Vera almost shouted. "What will happen when everyone gets here? They will all be looking at me, expecting me to say something. I can't just say: 'Good evening, the Papyrus is reopening.' And what am I supposed to serve

the guests? I have absolutely nothing. Even the glasses are locked in the back room. In any case—there
wouldn't be enough of them; only three or four, if I
remember correctly."

I could barely refrain from laughing at Vera's panic.

"Calm down. The author will take care of everything. I'm sure he didn't organize all this just to em-
barrass you."

"The author! If he doesn't appear soon—I'm out of
here, and then you can all deal with it however you want."

The bells rang again. A short young woman with a
snub nose entered, elegantly dressed in lively colors.
She gave us a brief smile, then headed towards the
bookshelves.

"You don't recognize her?" Vera asked me softly.

I shook my head.

"It's because of the hair. It wasn't medium length
and light brown, as it is now, but rather short and dark.
You saw her more than two years ago. She stood over
there," she indicated with her head, "next to the veteri-
nary student who died. You spoke to her."

"How can you remember what kind of hair some
woman had more than two years ago?"

"You're not the only one with a good memory. In
any case, what's difficult about it? She was a regular at
the Papyrus."

"You think that she was invited because of that?"

Vera shrugged. "I have no idea."

On the renewed ringing of the bells she looked at
me questioningly. Two men paused for a moment near
the entrance, as though unsure which direction to go
in, and then moved to the nearby corner. The older one
nodded to me, the younger one waved. I responded
with a slight bow.

"Former Chief Inspector Đorđević," I explained to
Vera in a low voice.

"He has a brief role in my novel too, but you don't

see him. Only a voice on the telephone. That's not how I imagined him."

"He retired after the 'Grand Manuscript' case. That's Inspector Jovan Petronijević with him. We shared an office during the 'Last Book' case. He passed on news from the Papyrus to the tabloids. That's why he's hesitant to come and say hello to you now."

"He looks like someone who has dealings with the tabloids."

"Excuse me for a moment; he might have similar ideas tonight."

I walked up to them and first cordially welcomed my former superior, then standoffishly greeted my colleague whom I had rarely seen since I had been given my own office. I pulled them aside for a moment.

"It might seem to you that tonight is an open house, but it isn't. People from the Agency are all around."

"No one asked me for an invitation at the entrance. Should I show it to you?"

"I mean someone who might come uninvited, because they've received word that no one is checking invitations."

"Who might that someone be?"

"I think we understand each other."

I patted him on the shoulder, then returned to the counter. I had just joined Vera, when the bells announced a new guest. I turned around and saw a short man with disheveled hair and a bushy mustache. The resemblance to Einstein was even greater than the first time I had seen him, in this same place. Professor Anatasije Nedeljković approached us boldly and in full flow.

"Dear Miss Gavilović! Dear Inspector Lukić! This is wonderful! The Papyrus is opening again! You've made me so happy! How I've missed it! It all comes down to this bookstore. This is where the solutions to all the secrets lie! I'll get right to work!"

He started going through the numerous pockets

of his coat and suit, looking for his famous notepad, but since it was nowhere to be found, he shrugged his shoulders mournfully and went to one of the corners to continue his search there.

Vera smiled as she watched him leave, then her face turned grim. "Where is the author?" she almost snarled at me. "There are more and more people."

As if to confirm this, the bells announced the arrival of a party of four: one woman and three men. The petite older woman in a gray coat and beret, as well as the gentleman in the plaid jacket, with an unlit pipe in his mouth, seemed vaguely familiar, but not the other two. The larger one was compensating for a complete absence of hair with a full beard, while the slimmer, shorter one wore a coat reaching almost to the ground.

"That's all I need right now," Vera whispered after giving the new arrivals a broad smile.

"What?" I asked, also softly.

"As though Einstein wasn't enough, the other patients were also invited. It's going to be interesting here tonight."

The lady with the beret sat down in one of the armchairs, took a small book out of her large handbag and started to read. The gentleman with the pipe quickly followed her example. He walked up to the bookshelves, chose a large book full of illustrations and sat down in the second armchair. The other two surveyed the situation in the bookstore, then headed in opposite directions and dived into browsing.

"Remember the old lady?"

"Is she the one who brings a collection of love poems to read here?"

Vera nodded.

"I think that I've seen the gentleman with the pipe too, but I'm not sure."

"You saw him the same time that you saw her—

during your second visit to the Papyrus. Whenever he comes in he looks at the same book with illustrations."

"You truly have a better memory than me. Now I'm impressed."

Vera bowed slightly. "I also mentioned the other two to you. The bald one with the beard always buys the same book. We've sold him nearly a hundred and fifty copies. The other one is probably concealing the volume that he has brought for us tonight. The longer the coat, the larger the book that he will leave on the shelf."

The bells this time announced the arrival of a larger group. Even though I saw these seven colleagues almost every day, I stared at them because I had never seen them dressed like this. Formal wear best became the new chief inspector, Vesna Uskoković. It also suited Grubijanić, the head of the laboratory, and Bumbaković, the young officer who worked the switchboard. Inspector Prokopović appeared quite uncomfortable in a suit, even though it looked good on him. Inspectors Kostić and Zarić seemed ill at ease, while the bow tie around the neck of the mustachioed Vranešević looked like a noose.

I stepped towards them, but the chief inspector signaled me to remain at the counter. They didn't stay together but rather scattered around the bookstore. Chief Inspector Uskoković stood with her predecessor, which finally freed him of Petronijević's company.

"My colleagues," I told Vera. "You know most of them from *The Grand Manuscript*. The lady is the new chief inspector, Vesna Uskoković, and that one over there," I nodded, "is Bubmaković, the switchboard operator."

I saw in Vera's eyes that she was preparing to say something about this invasion of police officers, but then her attention was completely consumed by the appearance of another colleague of mine at the entrance. I almost didn't recognize her. Ana Mirković always wore a ordinary white lab coat at work. She now looked very elegant, in a long black dress with an exceptionally low cut neckline and high heels. She smiled at me, then headed over to where her boss was standing.

"Let me guess," said Vera. "The young lab technician, who is interested in your literary recommendations, right?"

"How did you guess?"

"It wasn't difficult. She intentionally hung back at the door. She wouldn't have received the same attention if she had come in with a bunch of police officers as she did when she stepped in by herself. If you could only have seen how you stared at her. And then that smile she gave you. Certainly a sign of appreciation for an exceptional recommendation. Now you are connected by Saramago, and that is a strong bond. . . ."

"God, Vera. . . ." I said, but there was no opportunity to get into a discussion about Saramago being a pimp, because two new guests had just appeared at the door. A younger and an older lady were headed our way. I had never seen either of them before.

"Inspector Lukić, perhaps you will remember me," said the larger one, with the prominent double chin. She was already past fifty. "We spoke on the telephone. Leposava Žutić, from Magnifying Glass Press."

"How could I forget?"

"You weren't patient enough to hear our offer. . . ."

"You are lucky I didn't; it wasn't at all healthy to have anything to do with that manuscript."

She wanted to say something, but I turned to the younger woman. She was about thirty-five years old; her bangs fell over her eyebrows, and she wore an excessive amount of costume jewelry around her neck.

"I hope you haven't forgotten me either. Jelisaveta Šumanović, from *The Evening Courier*."

I started looking around for Petronijević.

"No one helped me get in," the reporter interrupted my search. "I'm here as a guest." She took out an elongated invitation and showed it to me. "However, if you want to give us an exclusive interview about the turbulent day behind you, whose finale we are attending. . . ."

"I can't, unfortunately. I'm here as an admirer of literature, not as a police inspector."

Miss Šumanović also wanted to continue our conversation, but she was thwarted by a fresh ringing of the bell.

"Excuse me," I said to the two ladies, as I walked around them and towards the door, where Mrs. Leleković, Mrs. Ognjanović and Mr. Vidojević stood, looking at the gathering in confusion.

"What is the meaning of this, Inspector Lukić?" asked the administrator of the City Cemeteries Administration. "It is quite inappropriate to invite people in mourning to a party."

"I didn't invite you. I myself am here because I was invited."

"So who invited everyone?"

"We still don't know, but we should find out soon."

"I certainly have no intention of waiting for that. My time is valuable."

"I would still recommend that you be patient. Perhaps you will no longer have reason to be in mourning."

She scowled at me. "What do you mean?"

There was no time to answer her, because the most conspicuous group so far had appeared at the bookstore entrance. The guests who had already arrived had stopped paying much attention to newcomers; it was as though only Vera and I were interested in who was arriving. This time, however, all heads turned to the entrance: led by the Grand Master, a procession of members of the secret society was filing into the Papyrus.

I reacted as quickly as I could under the circumstances. In great strides I rushed towards Vera, making my way around the people who stood between the door and the counter. They were slowing me down, but were also blocking the Grand Master from having a clear shot at his target, if he were to decide to fire immediately. From the corner of my eye I saw Kostić and Zarić quickly approach the counter from the left and right. I put my hand inside my jacket, ready to draw my gun.

We reached the register at the same time and stood in front of Vera like a human shield. As I turned around I faced a multitude of looks from guests who obviously didn't understand what had caused the sudden confusion. There was no threat to Vera or anyone else. The members of the secret society stood calmly in the corner farthest from the counter. The people who had previously been there had moved out of their way, giving them space.

After our two encounters in the dark that day, I finally had the opportunity to see the Grand Master. His tall stature made him stand out not only in the group around him, but also in the entire bookstore. He looked the same as he had the last time we had met, at the teashop eight months ago. His thick salt-and-pepper hair, pulled back in a pony tail, emphasized his high forehead and bony face, and the sparkle of the green jade in his eyes was simply captivating. He smiled at me for a split second when he caught me looking at him.

Six followers had come with him. The sister and brother who ran the teashop, the alleged cleaning lady Mrs. Sokolović, the woman who had impersonated attorney Jovana Timotijević, the girl who had first phoned me, then appeared before me when I was paralyzed, and the guard, Rabrenović.

I removed my hand from my jacket and whispered to Kostić and Zarić to back down, but the guests were still staring at me with discomfort. This would have continued, had the door bell not rung again. Almost everyone turned in that direction.

Finally arriving at the Papyrus were those who were actually supposed to have been here to begin with. A moment earlier, when the Grand Master and his band appeared, my first thought had been to wonder how they could have gotten past all the people from the Agency. I hadn't seen them, but nonetheless I was confident that they were keeping a close eye on the bookstore. Mirić would owe me some answers.

The eight young agents behaved just as the police officers had before them—they didn't stay together but rather scattered around the Papyrus. Mirić came to the counter.

"We are all here," Vera said excitedly from behind me. "There's no one else left."

I turned towards her. "How do you know?"

"Don't you get it? Everyone who appeared in the first two books was invited, with the exception of the dead, of course, and a few extras, such as the Oriental tea-shop proprietor and his twins. Everyone who has any significance in *The Last Book* and *The Grand Manuscript* is here. The author has brought together all his characters. He is the only one still missing."

I squinted long and hard at Vera, then started to shake my head. She looked back at me with confusion in her eyes.

"Actually, not everyone is here," I said in a low voice.

"Who's still not here? Who's missing?"

At that moment Mirić came up to me, leaned over and whispered in my ear: "We've determined whose handwriting is on the envelopes."

"I too have just deduced the same," I responded.

I didn't have the chance, however, to say anything because suddenly a loud gong sounded behind us.

THE SOUND HAD COME from the room behind the counter. In the general commotion I hadn't noticed that someone had unlocked the door and opened it wide. The chatter ceased instantly and everyone looked in that direction. For several moments nothing happened, then three figures, dressed in tight black pants and dark red Mandarin jackets, buttoned up to the top, emerged in quick succession. Each was carrying a large serving tray with a dozen blue-and-white steaming porcelain cups.

It was not unexpected that the older man with slanted eyes who headed the procession should have looked exactly the same as he had the last time I saw him, at the Mandarin Teashop: lean, with thinning hair, rheumatic movements. Two years barely made any difference at his age. A genuine transformation occurs, however, between the ages of twelve and fourteen. Yet by some miracle, it seemed as though the passage of time had had no effect on the teashop proprietor's twins. They also appeared unchanged, so I still couldn't distinguish which was the girl and which the boy.

They spread out in three directions among the guests, offering them tea with a smile and a bow. The trays with the many full cups must have been rather heavy for their small hands, but the children carried them seemingly effortlessly. The father made his way to the counter. As he approached us, he also bowed and gave us a wide smile.

"Miss Gavrilović, Inspector Lukić, meet again. Very pleased."

"We are pleased too," said Vera, as she took a cup. "We have greatly missed your teas."

"I especially missed the one for head work," I said, also taking a cup. "It could have spared me many headaches in the past two years."

"This one more good. Tea for ending."

"Tea for ending?" Vera repeated inquisitively, staring at the yellowish liquid. "What ending?"

"Happy ending. That always best."

Vera had already opened her mouth to continue questioning him but the teashop proprietor beat her to it. "You excuse me. Must take tea other guest. Should drink while hot."

He went around the counter, but then remembered something and came back to Vera. This time his voice was lower, and I could barely hear what he was saying.

"You wrong. I and children not extras. We important role. No happy ending without our tea."

Vera blushed as he continued toward the guests in the center of the bookstore with a renewed smile.

"How did he hear me?" she whispered when he was slightly further away.

"He probably has a tea for hear good. That's how he heard your lament about the refreshments earlier and rushed to help you out. Didn't I tell you that you shouldn't worry about it? The tea for ending certainly is more original than any of the typical things that are served at receptions."

Vera raised the cup to her lips, blew a little into the yellow liquid and sipped carefully. She remained straight-faced as she sampled the tea in her mouth, then she lit up.

"Marvelous. Go ahead and try it. It won't harm you."

It seemed to me that it was still scorching, but I couldn't disgrace myself. I took a modest gulp. The tea was truly magnificent. No single flavor was dominant. I had the impression that a plethora of indistinguishable ingredients were competing for precedence. First one prevailed, then another, toying with the taste buds.

"So?"

"It really is superb. The guests will be amazed. Actually, come to think of it, you and the mandarin could team up. Rent out the back room to him. You never used it for anything important. He can prepare teas there for your customers. Tea for read good, for example, or tea for buy book. Your business would flourish."

"You're joking at such a serious moment. Anyway, that topic is off the agenda; I am not going back to the Papyrus."

Having finished serving the refreshments, the father and children remained standing at three different places in the bookstore. With a smile, they held out the serving trays in front of them, waiting for the guests to place their empty cups on them. Under different circumstances Vera and I would have taken our time drinking this excellent beverage in small sips, but now we just downed it in silence. Mirić offered to take our cups to the nearest tray. I didn't notice what the other agents had done, but he did not have any tea.

"All right, let's hear it," said Vera.

"What?"

"Now that the mandarin and his twins are also here—who else is missing?"

"You don't have to be at all insightful in order to work it out. All it takes is to look around carefully yourself. Who is only person who is absent, and who should definitely be in the bookstore?"

Vera squinted at me, then got on her tiptoes and started scanning the guests. She had barely gotten through a quarter of the circle when the gong sounded again.

A three-person procession stepped out of the back room: a man in front, then a younger woman, and an older one. All had their hands full. He was carrying two large dark gray volumes; the woman behind him held a thick incunabulum, wearing plastic gloves; and the lady in the rear was pushing a wheelchair.

Excited voices came from the direction of the entrance and three figures started to push through the guests towards the newcomers. The old poet Vidojević was the first to make his way to his muse, but then he didn't know how to reach her since the wheelchair obstructed him. Finally, he leaned over and hugged her across it. Mrs. Ognjanović also had difficulties. She wanted to embrace her deputy, but the young woman backed away so that she could first raise the incunabulum above her head, and only then did she permit the hug. Only Mrs. Leleković did not have any difficulties. Even if he had wanted to, with his hands full the archivist could not resist her firm clutch. It was actually much firmer than might have been expected of the administrator, who was renowned for being very strict with her staff.

"The return of the three missing people," I explained to Vera.

"I understood. I just didn't expect the welcome to be so passionate in all three cases."

"Neither did I, although I should have guessed. It seems that necrophiliac passion brings people together as does biophiliac passion."

"Why did he take those two books of burials specifically?"

"To correct the mistakes in them."

Vera looked at me questioningly, but there was no time to explain, because another man had just emerged from the back room. Hardly anyone except me noticed him, because everyone was still preoccupied with the three embracing couples. I too would have failed to notice his appearance, had I not been facing in that direction. He walked straight towards us. Vera realized from my look that something was going on behind her and she quickly turned around.

"You don't have to continue seeking the missing person, Miss Gavrilović," said the elderly man in an overcoat. "We are finally all here."

"Commissioner Milenković! How could I have overlooked your absence? Unbelievable."

"There's quite a crowd at the Papyrus. It isn't easy to make out who all is here, let alone who is not. And Inspector Lukić realized who was missing only just before you did. In any case, had you noticed my absence earlier, it wouldn't have been good for the novel. Only now is it the right moment for me to appear."

"I could have figured out long ago who was behind all of this," I jumped in, "had I not relied on what you said."

"What I said?"

"During the 'Grand Manuscript' case, at one moment I proposed that you try to write detective novels. You resolutely responded that it was not for you, that you are more adept at solving than conceiving detective cases. Remember?"

"I remember. I still believe that."

"But you still started working on a novel?"

"I started working on it not because of my own motivation but at the author's incitement."

"He incited you to do something that you are not good at?"

"That's right. Being unskilled, I would be less suspicious, and he as a mentor made sure that my lack of talent wasn't obvious."

"Why did the author need you at all? Why didn't he write the novel himself?"

"He wanted to have two stories in the novel. One that would be in the foreground, and which someone else would write, and the other, his own, in the background, which would be best protected by the screen of the first story if it was penned by somebody else."

"Why did he choose to offer co-authorship to you? It can't just be because your ineptitude at writing would draw less suspicion. Many others meet that criteria."

"It was also convenient that I had retired. Everyone had lost track of me. The main reason, however, was the same that had previously led the author to help

Miss Gavrilović: he had done me wrong in the first two books. He felt guilty. He wanted to make amends."

"He had done you wrong? How is that?"

"You of all people should know. You were his main accomplice. No one had ever strung along a National Security Agency commissioner like the two of you did."

"How could he make amends for that?"

"He offered me the opportunity to string someone along too."

I looked silently at him for several moments.

"Me?"

"To tell you the truth, I would rather have taken the author for a ride than you, but that was a pleasure I couldn't really have hoped for."

"So, that was your main motivation in picking up the quill? Bruised ego? Revenge?"

"Very benevolent revenge. I had to show you a little what it is like when you keep smashing your head against unsolvable riddles everywhere you turn."

"As though I didn't already know. The author took me for a ride as much as he did you."

"Yet you came out as the winner in the end."

"And what about the Grand Master? He certainly strung you along a lot more than I did, and you didn't take any revenge on him. Your young colleagues believe that someone is protecting him. Might that be you?"

"I'm not nearly that powerful. Only the author himself could protect him. He needed such a character. It seems that he is inevitable in this type of novel. However, we will soon be getting rid of him too. Permanently."

"Him too? Who else?"

Commissioner Milenković sighed.

"What you said, that my main motivation was bruised ego and revenge—it hurt me. I thought you knew me better. The collaboration with the author would never had happened had he not made me an of-fer I simply couldn't refuse."

"What was it?"

"He promised that this would be his last involve-ment in our reality. I would have agreed to anything for such an outcome. Crossing realities are the worst possible nightmare that the National Security Agency has ever faced."

"That's not your concern any more; you're retired."

"Don't be naive, Inspector Lukić. There's no retire-ment in this line of work."

"The author made the same promise first to Dejan, then to me," Vera interjected. "And he never kept it. It is also naive to believe the promises of an author."

"He will keep it this time."

"What guarantees do you have?" I asked.

"The finale of this novel."

"Finale? I hope you don't mean the return of these three missing people?" I indicated the group that was still the focus of the guests' attention.

Commissioner Milenković shook his head. "No, of course not. That's just the conclusion of my story in the novel."

"You really put those three couples through hell in order to get back at me."

"They have no reason to complain. Everyone has been compensated for the anguish that they suffered. Mrs. Leleković and Mr. Trpimirović have finally bonded; they couldn't really achieve that at the City Cemeteries Administration. Mrs. Ognjanović and Miss Šuvaković have acquired an exceptionally rare in-cunabulum; they will have a little trouble explaining where they got it, but I'm sure they will manage. Fi-nally, Mr. Vidojević's penance has ended; his muse can walk and speak again."

"So, the finale of the author's story?"

"That's right, the story because of which *The Com-*

pendium of the Dead was written in the first place. The finale toward which lead the clues the author has sprinkled for the insightful inspector throughout the novel." He paused for a moment. "Now you can guess what comes next, right?"

I remained staring at Commissioner Milenković for several moments, then nodded.

"I can."

"I can't guess," said Vera.

"I know. You are not yet supposed to be able to guess. I have still to prepare you for the finale. There is great elation ahead for you."

"What elation?" Vera asked after a brief hesitation.

"I believe you are aware that the author is a very orderly person. Before he leaves our world for good, he wants to clean up the disorder that he has created, to restore the order that existed at the beginning of *The Last Book*."

"Not everything can be cleaned up," said Vera in a soft, shaking voice. "Unfortunately there are unfixable disorders. . . ."

Up to that moment I was convinced that I would never see a smile on the commissioner's face.

"Is a pitiful retired agent of the secret police supposed to enlighten you—you who live in the world of books—about the power of literature?"

Vera did not have a chance to respond because there was a commotion among the guests. The teashop proprietor and his twins had collected all the empty cups and were on their way through the crowd towards the back room. They had just stepped in there when the gong sounded for a third time. Everyone looked towards the door, expecting someone to emerge, but no one did. Instead the lights started to fade.

Once the room had grown dim, nothing happened for a brief while. Then the silence that had fallen on the guests started to fill with a murmur similar to a prayer or mantra. It took me several moments to make out that it was coming from the corner where the members of the secret society were standing, and a bit longer to realize why it sounded familiar: slightly over two years ago I had heard it in the underground hall of a villa. . . .

The mantra subsided at the moment when something suddenly started to glow on the wall opposite the entrance. At first it seemed to me that it came from several vertical lamps emitting a white light and placed one next to the other in the middle of the highest row of shelves—but I was wrong. The glow was from the spines of four white books that I hadn't noticed previously, because they were hidden among other volumes with white covers.

The four books that had finally come together—*The Compendium of the Dead.*

The glow rapidly increased in intensity, bathing the bookstore in blazing whiteness. I squinted, and a number of hands were raised to protect eyes. It seemed inevitable that the source of light would shatter, but the opposite happened—it suddenly died away. In the restored semidarkness the afterimage of four spines lingered for a while, creating the illusion that they were still high up on the shelf. However, when my eyes adjusted to the dim light, I saw that there was a gaping void where the books had been.

I gave the members of the secret society an inquisitive look and noticed another disappearance. Among the penitently bowed heads, the tallest one, crowned with salt-and-pepper hair, was missing. There was no time, however, to wonder what had happened to the books and the Grand Master. The lighting on the ceiling started to grow brighter, and a fourth gong sounded from the back room.

All heads turned in that direction once again. For a brief moment nothing moved. Then a short old man in a green overcoat appeared at the door. He looked around the bookstore bewildered, as though awakened from a restless sleep, still not able to figure out where he was. The sheer number of curious gazes directed at him caused additional confusion. Not knowing what else to do, he remained at the door, squinting.

I took Vera by the hand. "Do you recognize him?" I asked in a whisper.

She turned towards me and looked deep into my eyes, then made an unclear motion with her head that could at the same time be both nodding and shaking; both denial and agreement.

"Mr. Predrag Todorović?" she said in a whisper.

"Yes, the retired piano teacher."

"But he is. . . ."

"Dead. Yes, but not anymore."

"How. . . .?"

"Does it matter? Go to him."

This time Vera just fiercely shook her head.

"There's no one else," I said softy. "You are the only person here whom he knows. Should no one greet him upon his return from the dead? Look how baffled he is."

Her gaze stabbed me in the eyes once again. I let go of her hand, then smiled.

"Go on."

She started out with a uncertain step. She stopped in front of the old man, observed him briefly, then began to speak to him. She had her back to me so I couldn't make out the hushed words, but I saw their effect on the professor's face. The convulsion of bewilderment slowly thawed into an expression of confidence, which eliminated the need for unnecessary questions and answers.

He let her put her arm about him and walk him to the other end of the bookstore. The guests considerately cleared a path for them. He only hesitated a little before sitting down in the armchair where he had forever closed his eyes twenty-six months earlier. All it took was a light squeeze of Vera's hand to convince him that that forever had already passed.

Having settled him there, she returned just as a new figure appeared at the door to the back room. Vera smiled at me in passing and continued on to greet retired painter Ljubica Matić. The old woman was in a thin dark coat, with a purple scarf around her neck.

The second encounter was shorter than the first. The painter nodded at everything Vera said, as though she was telling her something ordinary, something that was a given. She only said something once at which they both laughed. They continued the talk in the same manner as they walked over to the last free armchair.

Vera also went to meet the third newcomer, but a young brunette was nearer and swifter. She quickly made her way though the crowd to the young man with the bright-red scarf. They didn't say a word. They held hands and stood there for a minute, gazing at each other. Then they went towards the shelf next to which he had once collapsed. There she first whispered something to him, then he whispered to her and then he touched the large earring in his left ear.

When the fourth person appeared at the back room door I restrained Vera, who had joined me in the meantime.

"But that was our highly revered customer," she protested. "Mrs. Dragana Stojanović, curator of the Museum of Modern Art. . . ."

"Someone else longs to greet her."

I nodded in the direction of the corner that Professor Nedeljković had retreated to. He was already making his way through the guests, waving his notepad in the air. After reaching Mrs. Stojanović, he showered her with a torrent of words, not allowing her to say anything. He kept flipping through his notepad, proudly pointing with his finger to different places in it. Finally he more or less dragged the curator to his corner.

"We should have spared the poor woman the experience," Vera said grimly. "She could live to regret coming back to life."

"The poor woman was herself a patient. There is no greeting more fitting for her. He will convince her to accept her resurrection more easily than you would."

A short stout red-haired woman with a large purse and big glasses emerged from the back room. She wore a colorful poncho over her beige blouse.

"In this case I have to welcome her back to the land of the living. Miss Ljubica Aksentijević might be one of the characters from your novel, but you are a stranger to her. Of all the people gathered here, she knows only me." I paused and turned to Commissioner Milenković. "No, I'm mistaken. She also met with you."

"Only briefly. I think that she has fonder memories of you. Please go ahead."

With a big smile I went up to the literary agent.

"Good evening, Miss Aksentijević."

"Inspector Lukić. . . ." she responded after a little hesitation, as though she hadn't recognized me immediately.

"How are you feeling?"

"Somehow deadened . . . as though. . . ." She left the sentence unfinished, looking at me helplessly.

I took her by the arm and patted her hand.

"Don't worry. Everything will be all right. I'm sure that you're just a little tired."

"Forgive me, could you tell me where we are? I'm very embarrassed, I can't remember. . . ."

"It's not a big deal. It happens to everyone. We are at a reception at a bookstore."

"The presentation of a new book?" Her voice perked up a little.

I hesitated for a moment. "Well, you could say so. . . ."

"A well-known author?"

"Not exactly. . . ."

"Do they have an agent?"

"I don't think so."

"Do you know them?"

"Yes, in a way. . . ."

"Could you introduce me?"

"Gladly, as soon as the program is finished."

"I'll wait. I'm already feeling better."

She smiled, then mingled with the guests.

I had just rejoined Vera, when a short man with graying hair and a thin mustache, wearing an elegant dark suit and bow tie, emerged from the room. Had I known that Inspector Tanasije Vesić would be the next one coming out, I would have stayed by the door. I had not returned there, however, which is why Commissioner Milenković beat me to him.

"I'll get this," he said shortly.

He approached the inspector and without any gestures, not even a handshake, entered into a muffled conversation. Someone uninformed would never have guessed that it was a welcome for a man who had just risen from the dead. The scene looked like the encounter of two friends at a reception, exchanging thoughts about something confidential, but harmless. It didn't last very long. In the end, having nodded in the direction of Vera and me, Vesić headed towards where chief inspectors Đorđević and Uskoković stood. Milenković came back to the counter.

"I invited him to join the Agency," he said softly. "He is all round a valuable man, and especially now, with this posthumous experience."

"What did he say?"

"That he would think about it. He said that this experience has changed his priorities a bit."

When the blond and stout Dr. Sonja Vidić appeared at the door of the back room, wearing heavy makeup despite the circumstances, Dr. Dimitrijević was already

ready to step in. He went up to her, and without saying a word placed his fingers against her carotid artery. As though that wasn't enough, he first grabbed her left, then her right hand and checked her pulse.

He then pelted her with medical questions. He fired them one after another in quick succession, not giving her an opportunity to answer. Dr. Vidić finally stopped the torrent by placing her hand over his mouth.

"I'm alive." She uttered the irrefutable diagnosis.

He silently stared at her for several moments, and then it was as though his face shattered: the man professionally numbed by death was brought to tears by life. Dr. Vidić embraced him and started to whisper something to him. They remained like that for some time, only for her to take him aside finally, her arm around his shoulders.

Vera grabbed my upper arm.

"Let's go, Dejan. Stay with me."

We went to the door of the back room, to greet the last, eighth person to return from the dead. I could tell how anxious Vera was by the involuntary twitching of her fingers.

We stopped in front of the door and peered inside. All we could see was a thick darkness. Seconds passed, long and tense, but no one emerged. At one moment Vera turned her head and gave me a confused look. I stroked her hand.

When someone finally appeared, it wasn't only Olga. She was holding by the arm an older man with round wire-framed glasses. They were both smiling.

"Good evening, Vera," said the author with a bow. "Good evening, Dejan."

We both returned the bows.

"Here we are at the end," the author continued. "I had to come to say goodbye. It wouldn't have been nice of me not to appear, would it?"

"I'm glad that you came," Vera responded. "I should

thank you for all this." She pointed to the bookstore, then with a smile nodded towards Olga.

"I promised that I wouldn't leave any damage in your world behind me, and above all that there wouldn't be any deaths."

"Won't you suffer damage because of that? Fans of detective novels tend to be bloodthirsty. They might not appreciate your vegetarian thrillers."

"I'm not worried by the bloodthirsty readers. Let them look elsewhere for what suits them. There are plenty of books of that kind."

"And you really won't be coming back?"

"I would just spoil everything with a fourth part, now that everything is brought to a close and settled." He paused for a moment. "Not everything, actually; there is just one more detail that I need to restore to what it was before. Unfortunately that concerns you, Vera."

"I was hoping you would forget that."

"What kind of a thriller writer would I be—even if I do write vegetarian ones—if I were to forget the details?"

"Should I close my eyes?"

"That would be easiest."

Vera looked around her. Before she closed her eyes, a shadow passed across her face.

She opened them a moment later, then looked around the bookstore and smiled. "The good old black-and-white Papyrus. . . ."

"Goodbye, Vera." He kissed her on both cheeks, then turned towards me and put out his hand. "Dejan." He finally nodded to Olga. "Miss Bogdanović."

He waved to the guests, then stepped into the darkness of the back room without waiting to hear their applause.

I stood patiently with Vera and Olga until they finally separated after their long hug.

"I'm very sorry, Vera, that nothing will come of your painting," I said. "I hope that running the Papyrus with Olga once more will be compensation enough."

"Why wouldn't I paint?"

I looked at her with a raised eyebrow. "Well, because you are colorblind again. . . ."

Vera smiled. "Yes, but I remember colors. . . ."

Contributors

About the author

Zoran Živković was born in Belgrade, Serbia, on October 5, 1948. Until his retirement in 2017, he was a full professor at the Faculty of Philology, the University of Belgrade, teaching creative writing.

He is one of the most translated contemporary Serbian writers: by the end of 2021 there were 117 foreign editions of his books of fiction, published in 24 countries, in 20 languages.

Živković has won several literary awards for his fiction. In 1994 his novel *The Fourth Circle* won the Miloš Crnjanski award. In 2003, Živković's mosaic novel *The Library* won a World Fantasy Award for Best Novella. In 2007 his novel *The Bridge* won the Isidora Sekulić award. In 2007 Živković received the Stefan Mitrov Ljubiša award for his life achievement in literature. In 2014 and 2015 Živković received three awards for his contribution to the literature of fantastika: Art-Anima, Stanislav Lem and The Golden Dragon.

Zoran Živković has been recognized with his selection as European Grand Master for 2017 by the European Science Fiction Society at the 39th Eurocon in Dortmund, Germany.

Živković is the author of 23 books of fiction:

About the artist

Youchan Ito was born 1968 in Aichi prefecture, Japan. She launched her career as a graphic designer in 1988, becoming a freelancer illustrator in 1991 and founding Togoru Co., Ltd. with her husband in 2000. In 2017 the company was reborn as Togoru Art Works. Handles a wide range of genres including cover art and design for science fiction, mysteries and horror titles, as well as illustrations for children's books.

www.youchan.com